DOUBLE FEATURE

PRESENTS

ASCENDENT

Bienvenue au Grand Guignol!!!!

Un Message Du Fondateur et La Vicomtesse

WELCOME BACK MY FRIENDS, TO THE SHOW THAT NEVER ENDS; WE'RE SO GLAD YOU COULD ATTEND. COME INSIDE, COME INSIDE."

\- EMERSON, LAKE, AND PALMER

Le FOUNDATEUR:

"Here we are then, gathered outside the Theatre du Grand Guignol awaiting entry to take part in a one-of-a-kind evening of entertainment and spectacle that only this unique arena could promise and then deliver upon. Some of you here know exactly what you are in for – and to those enlightened patrons we bid you move to front of the line so that we may show you to your seats quicker. No doubt your thirst and…shall we say desires will be sated and met this evening. Allow us to address those that have come unknowing anc unfamiliar with history and reputation of the Grand Guignol, and as such are unaware of the…effect of the ten plays they are about to read and thus imagine will have on their minds, their psyche, and with any luck, their souls."

La VICOMTESSE:

"Alright, the rest of you lot. *Faites attention.*

The Theatre du Grand Guignol (theatre of the great puppet) was a venue built out of an old church in the Pigalle District of Paris. The Pigalle (yes, ha-ha Pig Alley, you're not the first to think of that) was and is known for its multitude of sex shops, adult shows and the like even to this day. Soldiers in World War II would frequent the area for just that purpose, but well before that horrific period European history, the Grand Guignol opened its doors in 1897.

The Grand Guignol specialized in incredibly gory, graphic, and amoral horror plays and productions – with an emphasis on maintaining a naturalistic perspective on the proceedings. Meaning, the plays that were shown were acted and staged in such a way as to be a realistic as possible. So when one uses the adjectives "gory" and "graphic" in one sentence, and then follows it up in the next with "realistic", it meant that the plays that were shown at the Grand Guignol were some seriously fucked up pieces of theatre.

There was fake blood. And lots of it.

The actors and actresses were coached to and portrayed their characters as really having their eyes gouged out, fingers cut off, brains scooped out of their heads, and so on. The Grand Guignol was a night of anywhere from 6 -8 short plays that rolled out more like live action snuff films more than stage productions.

Have I mentioned the completely perverted, sexual overtones to the violence as well? No? Oh, well that too."

Le FOUNDATEUR (returning):

"Did you get to the sexy part yet?"

La VICOMTESSE:

"Alright, the rest of you lot. *Faites attention.*

The Theatre du Grand Guignol (theatre of the great puppet) was a venue built out of an old church in the Pigalle District of Paris. The Pigalle (yes, ha-ha Pig Alley, you're not the first to think of that) was and is known for its multitude of sex shops, adult shows, and the like even to this day. Soldiers in World War II would frequent the area for just that purpose, but well before that horrific period i European history, the Grand Guignol opened its doors in 1897.

The Grand Guignol specialized in incredibly gory, graphic, and amoral horror plays and productions – with an emphasis on maintaining a naturalistic perspective on the proceedings. Meaning, the plays that were shown were acted and staged in such a way as to be a realistic as possible. So when one uses the adjectives "gory" and "graphic" in one sentence, and then follows it up in the next with "realistic", it meant that the plays that were shown at the Grand Guignol were some seriously fucked up pieces of theatre.

There was fake blood. And lots of it.

The actors and actresses were coached to and portrayed their characters as really having their eyes gouged out, fingers cut off, brains scooped out of their heads, and so on. The Grand Guignol was a night of anywhere from 6 -8 short plays that rolled out more like live action snuff films more than stage productions.

Have I mentioned the completely perverted, sexual overtones to the violence as well? No? Oh, well that too."

Le FOUNDATEUR (returning):

"Did you get to the sexy part yet?"

La VICOMTESSE:

"Non, mon ami. C'est tout a toi."

Le FOUNDATEUR:

No joke – there were boxes towards the back of the floor that the upper crust could reserve on any particular evening. These boxes, back when the theatre was a church (!!) used to be where the nuns would sit in while masses were conducted. During the Grand Guignol and its heyday, the boxes were used as not-so secret fuck boxes. That's right children– the same places where Sister Marguerite and Sister Cezanne would sit and penitently listen to a priest give benedictions at one time would eventually become the shagging section for those so turned on by a woman having her hoo-ha scooped out they simply had to get their holes filled that very same moment. It even became a running joke - when the fucking got too loud even for the performers, the entire stage and rest of the audience would stop altogether and shout: *gardez-le-la-dedans!* (Keep it down in there).

Back in oh, October, the Double Feature staff decided that we would do an "annual" issue, a double-sized, free-for-all, themed edition. But, we couldn't just do a Double Double Feature, that would be redundant. So, figuring that the magazine was ostensibly a tribute to 50s, 60s, and 70s Grindhouse and Drive-In Theatres and that wonderful format that has become such a calling card of American culture, why not pattern the annual issue over something similar, some forgotten chestnut of mayhem and the macabre, of trash and the titillating, of splatter and the sexy. The answer was quite clear to us – we would present to you, the reader, *An Evening at the Grand Guignol.*

For this evening, you may regard us as *Le Foundateur* ("The Founder") and *La Vicomtesse* ("The Viscountess") of this twisted troupe of authors, artists, and creators. We have banded together to bring you ten tales of the terrifying and mystifying, dripping with profanity and insanity and heresy and hypocrisy so outrageous and ostentatious your mind's eyes will burn with hellfire for the hours and the days and the weeks to come. So, without any further *battage*…"

La VICOMTESSE:

"Zut alors, ton Francais est nul."

Le FOUNDATEUR:

"Well, thank you partner! We begin tonight with the tale of a simple girl trying to make her way in the world…

La VICOMTESSE:

"and a very, VERY special pair of shoes..."

Le FOUNDATEUR (closes entry doors. Lowers head, and looks down at ground)

La VICOMTESSE (places hand on Le FOUNDATEUR's shoulder)

"C'est bon, mon frere?"

Le FOUNDATEUR:

"Maintenant."

La VICOMTESSE:

"You're lying."

Le FOUNDATEUR (turning, a false smile, eyes of ghosts, spectres):

"Maintenant."

La VICOMTESSE:

"Come, once more then. Let's give them a night…"

Le FOUNDATEUR:

"That will psychically damage all who look upon its horrors?"

La VICOMTESSE:

"To remember, Wally."

Le FOUNDATEUR:

"Same fucking thing, dude"

La VICOMTESSE:

"So refreshing when you return to the truth with such flourish."

Le FOUNDATEUR and La VICOMTESSE enter the doors….and then the audience's screaming begins.

ASCENDENT

Greetings, and welcome to our homage to the Grand Guignol! This is not a place for the unwary or ill-informed. You see, our writers are bloodthirsty, savage maniacs, and if you are not thoroughly prepared, you might come away from our little show sickened to your very core. And while that may, indeed, be our very aim, I feel it is only fair to warn you first. My own story contains sexual perversions of a strange and frankly horrifying nature. As such, I have been named "It" and am the one tasked with warning you, our audience. So, without further ado, here is an inexhaustive list of potentially disturbing occurrences that may be found within:

Dismemberment
Infanticide
Suicide
Bestiality
Onanism
Drug Use
Alcohol Use
Murder
Human Experimentation
Blasphemy
Mental Illness (Chronic)
Racism
Hate Crime
And possibly more...

So, now that you are prepared, please do come inside. Find a seat and settle in for an experience like none other. An evening at The Grand Guignol!

-SN Humphreys
Directeur, Le Jardin de Gomorrhe

PROGRAMME
DE CAUCHEMARS

Un. Grenats et Cuir

English title: "Garnets & Leather" **Melody Alice**

Deux. Le Baiser de Minuit

English title: "Champagne" **wp Quigley**

Trois. Feu de Benne

English title: "Dumpster Fire" **D.S. Vernon**

Quatre. Le Jardin de Gomorrhe

English title: "The Garden of Gomorrah" **S.N. Humphreys**

Cinq. Les Falcons De La Nuit

English title: "Nighthawks" **John A. McColley**

Six. Et Les Doux Heriteront . . .

English title: "No Pain" **Madi Quinn**

Sept. L'Heritage De La Fille

English title: "Pockabook" **Maggie Moreau**

Huit. Meme Les Monstres Font Des Cauchemars

English title: "Monsters Have Nightmares Too" **Michael Strong**

Finale. Mimes Sur La Seine

English title: "Mimes on the Seine" **Lucienne LeBeau**

Grenats et Cuir

Directour: Melody Alice

UN SPECTACLE D'HORREUR EN CINQ ACTES SANS MERCI

COMMENCE A' 20H SUIVI "LE BAISER DE MINUIT" "FEU DE BENNE"
"LE JARDIN DE GOMORRHE" ET "LES FALCONS DE LA NUIT"

Acte Un.

They were still there. Waiting.

That's how she'd liked to think of them, as waiting. Just for her. She'd been saving up to buy them for months now. All that time…waiting.

They were the most perfect vintage shoes. From what she could see of their condition, displayed in the shop window facing the street, they weren't just lovely. They were pristine. All the while, during which she would save a dollar here, a couple of quarters there, the shoes remained miraculously unsold. It was as if they weren't waiting just for her, they *wanted* to be hers. That's also how she liked to think of them; that they wanted to belong to her. She wanted to belong to them in kind.

The interior of the head shop that had the shoes on display always looked and smelled the same. The air was thick with an ever-present mixture of Nag Champa, old denim, and a bloody metallic smell. She assumed this last came from the dusty collection of rusty wrought iron fixtures at the back of the store and the not-unpleasant-on-its-own smell of dust and old paper from the used books area. And beneath all those aromas, there was an undercurrent in the final perfume that might have been the moldy old building itself - slightly wet and rotten, a smell that no amount of incense or old metal could cover up completely.

She went into the shop once a week to surreptitiously ogle the shoes, *her* shoes. Each visit ended up as a few minutes of pretending to browse the various wares, but then always leaving empty-handed. It had become no surprise that when the shopkeeper glanced towards the door when the bell above it rang, he returned his attention to his paperback the moment he saw that girl who never bought anything, ever, enter his store.

Today was different. Today, she'd finally accumulated enough disposable income so that her prize could - and would finally be hers. In the afternoon, she went straight to the head shop, straight to the window display and grabbed the shoes, feeling an electric charge shoot through her skin at how perfect they felt in her hands.

Prior to that moment, she had never touched them before. As a rule, she would never touch anything she couldn't afford, and until today that included her shoes. It was ….

…worth the wait. It was worth the work. They were so soft, the leather well-worn yet somehow appearing and feeling brand-new, with not a scuff nor a defect to be found or felt.

The shopkeeper's eyebrows lifted when she placed them on the counter and dug her wallet out of her bag. He stood up from the stool he had been perched upon and peered over the counter at her current footwear - a pair of visibly worn Doc Marten boots. The sour expression that he always wore mutated into full disdain as his eyes traveled up from the boots to her torn fishnets, then reaching her black velvet babydoll dress. He lingered a little too long on her chest before finally meeting her eyes with his own.

"You sure these are even going to fit you? Your feet don't exactly look…." he trailed off, nodding down to her boots as if that explained anything.

"They'll fit," she mumbled, averting her eyes as she held the cash out to him. *What a creep*, she thought. She took comfort in knowing that once she had the shoes, she'd never have to come back to this place again.

His sticky, sweaty hand unpleasantly brushed hers as the money was snatched from her palm. He pushed the shoes unceremoniously towards her on the counter between them. Before she knew it, she was back out on the street, shoes in hand. He hadn't even given her a bag. She didn't even slightly care about this final act of inconsideration. She raced home to try them on, heart pounding with excitement.

Acte Deux.

The very next night, she wore the shoes out to the clubs. At first, she was worried a bit about damaging them on such a risky excursion, but she reasoned that it would be fine, just this one time, to show them off to her friends. She never danced when she went to the clubs, so there were no worries about getting them stepped on or worn down. And the shoes had already proven to be far from delicate - despite their age. She parked her car in the downtown parking lot, so it was just a matter of a few steps taken in the outdoor elements and on the unforgiving and broken pavement before she'd be inside wherever the chosen destination was. Then she'd be parked at her group's usual table drinking, gossiping, and watching the dancers…

on the floor fluttering about like moths gathered in front of neon lights.

Daphne noticed the new shoes first. "Oh! Those are just lovely. Where *did* you find them?" As Daphne extended her hand to touch her left shoe, she instinctively and reflexively moved her foot away, crossing her ankles underneath the table. The quickness with which she executed this movement surprised her friend.

"Oh wow," Daphne said with an affronted snort, rolling her eyes, though her projected countenance of insult failed to conceal her hurt. How could she explain to Daphne that she just didn't want anyone else touching them without sounding mean?

Sheepishly, she slowly put her legs back out, doing little kicks with her feet to ensure all her friends could see how the rhinestones on the buckles and T-strap sparkled in the frantic lighting of the club. All at once, three pairs of hands shot out. She wanted to pull away again but held on, letting their hands lightly touch the shoes. Daphne sat obstinate, with her arms folded and still quite incensed from the interaction just moments before.

The rest of her friends squealed with delight, and she felt a warm thrill of satisfaction. It was hard to impress this crowd. Most of them, ok, ALL of them, had more disposable income than she did. She didn't think she'd ever seen any of them wear the same outfit out twice to the club.

"1940s aesthetic, I assume?" Daphne cocked her head, to listen for her response.

"Obviously 1920s. That buckle has Art Deco practically stamped on it," Percy sneered, before she could respond.

"No. Older! *Fin de Siècle.* Obviously. The heel is too low and curved for the flapper era," another interjection, this time from Mara, and punctuated with an eyeroll.

She had no idea what the hell they were talking about. She was pretty sure they didn't either, but this was their normal routine. Their snobbish debates. But this time it was playful, all three of them smiling, their usual bored expressions wiped clean as they kept glancing down at her feet. The dim flicker of the candle at the center of their table reflected the rhinestone sparkles in all their eyes, making

Maybe it was also the smoke in the club. The haze of cloves and evaporating sweat made her friends' expressions change and flicker like a silent film. Tragedy and comedy masks. First happy and open, and then leering and sad. Back and forth, all while they laughed and kept reaching out to stroke her shoes. She laughed with them, kicking her feet a bit for them as they grabbed at her, and each time they grabbed she seemed to have been throwing back the last of another cocktail.

Acte Trois.

She woke up late the next morning, still in her club outfit, lipstick and mascara smeared on her pillow. As she lifted her head, pounding from countless gin and tonics imbibed the night before, she spotted her shoes in the corner of the room and smiled to herself. She just knew one of her friends would have some amazing new bauble to show off by next week, maybe even sooner. A forgotten family heirloom, something decadent dug out of some long-passed relative's moldering trunk, or a one-of-a-kind piece from a trendy uptown designer that specialized in their groups' very particular and very dark aesthetic. Whatever the futile attempt to mimic her new footwear *mode d'emploi* ended up manifesting itself as, it wouldn't matter. These shoes were just for her.

She finally had one special thing of her own. She squinted as an email notification caught her attention, displayed in a large font on her computer screen. She didn't need to get up to open it. She could see just from the notification all that mattered about it. It was her agent, passing on news of yet another rejection. Her morning mood already ruined, she then almost sadistically glanced at the small stack of bills on the nightstand.

Fuck, she thought grimly to herself. As much as she enjoyed them, and as meticulously as she had saved her money, the shoes still were an irresponsible purchase. She had no real steady income to speak of - and the rejection she'd just seen was a jarring reminder of that fact of her existence. Maybe she could return them and get her money back, but she knew that was a long shot. Shops like that didn't do refunds, and that hideous man hadn't even given her a bag, let…

…alone a receipt.

She looked back to the shoes.

Wait.

What was that…a mark on the right one? She squinted, her head banging away like a jackhammer and her vision blurry. Yes, there was a worn bit, a patch where the color on the leather was a bit lighter.

Double fuck, she thought.

She hopped out of bed and stumbled immediately, annoyed at both the shoes and herself. Sure enough, the black leather wasn't quite black on the back right heel. It looked more like oxblood. She rubbed the spot with her index finger and more of the shoes' original black seemed to come off with her prodding. Had they been dyed?

She should have known. That shop owner was not only a creep, but a crook.

She grumbled as she took the shoes to the bathroom to see them better in the bright lights installed over the sink. In that smaller space, she could smell herself. There was the familiar, morning-after-a-club-night mixture of perfume oil, sweat, and smoke. But beneath that, there was another scent that wasn't her own. Metallic. Like the metallic smell she'd detect when -

She checked to make sure her cycle hadn't come early. It hadn't. So where then, was this smell of newly liberated blood coming from?

Her eyes flicked down to the shoes on the counter. She slowly lifted one and sniffed. No. Just old leather. She lifted the damaged shoe and sniffed at the worn spot. There it was. That close, it lost its metallic tang and instead took on the olfactory traits of rotten fruit. Pulpy, and rich.

Recoiling, she put the shoes beneath the sink countertop, containing their smell in the bathroom cabinet. She showered and rinsed her mouth quickly, swallowed two Percocet, and returned to bed, drifting back to sleep when the opiates hit her system and took hold of her pain receptors.

She woke up to a dark apartment. The headache and the painkillers had knocked her out for a full day. She felt around for her phone in the bed. Picking it up, swiping it on, and then blinding herself with the screen's light, she saw that she had missed a barrage of texts and calls…

…from her friends. It was unusual for any of them to contact her at all, let alone these many times in a single day. None of them were the "chat on the phone" types. Their weekly meetups at the club were all the social time they needed, and by that point in their collective relationships they could each count on the others to be present, prior contact or no. So, what the hell was this? There must have been some kind of emergency to warrant all of this. She popped out of bed and double checked the time on her phone. Almost midnight. They'd all been texting her since four am the night before, almost as soon as she'd arrived home and had already passed out. The messages started coming in one-hour intervals at first, increasing in frequency as the day and then night wore on.

What the hell is going on here, she thought as she scrolled through their messages. There wasn't an emergency. They were all just individually checking on her at first, making the kind of boring small talk that wasn't at all like them.

Did you make it home alright? said one.

Wow I've never seen you down that many cocktails, girl, said another.

She couldn't recall a time when any of them had checked in on her to make sure that she had arrived home safely.

This is nice guys, but a little strange, she thought. More than a little. A lot strange.

She kept scrolling. The messages shifted in content from her wellbeing to her shoes. Debates about the origins of the shoes. Would she be wearing them next week? Would she like to go out shopping? Would she like to come over for a drink at their house? With the shoes, of course. Always a mention of the shoes. Their messages were all sent separately, but all eerily similar. At last, she turned her phone off, dismayed at the bizarre nature of their collective behavior.

It occurred to her at that moment:

The shoes had a greater effect on her friends than they had on her.

The thought made her mind reel, the acceptance of it as truth made her sense of balance do the same. She nearly fell to the ground from the feeling of vertigo the messages had instilled in her.

Water. She needed water. She was…

. . . parched and her mouth felt dry and cobwebby and gross from sleep. She went to the bathroom to brush her teeth and as she opened the door, the smell hit her like a wave that struck a person with their back turned to it. It was both the metallic and the rotten fruit scents combined into one overpowering stench.

She opened the cabinet, wherein the concentrated smell had grown so strong that she gagged on the spot. The shoes had left a stain on the white cabinet. They looked like they had melted, the dye running off and pooling at the edges. It looked like filthy rainwater on dark pavement.

"Oh, the landlord is going to love this!" she groused, snatching them up and tossing them on the much easier to clean tile floor.

The shoes squeaked as they skidded and left a reddish-brown smear across the floor. She stared at the damage. After a moment, she dipped her trembling finger into the smear left by the shoes. She tentatively brought it to her nose, then her mouth, tongue darting out, licking quickly like she was afraid of being caught in the act of doing so.

Her eyes saucered the instant the liquid touched but a single taste bud. It wasn't dye.

It was blood. The shoes were weeping blood. Stupidly, she looked down at her feet. Intact with no scrapes or blisters.

"What. The. Fuck." she whispered.

Her hands were still shaking after she had double bagged the shoes in plastic grocery bags and thrown them back inside the cabinet. She quickly cleaned up the crimson-colored evidence, haphazardly sprinkling her too-expensive-to-be-sprinkling perfume oil all around the bathroom like a Catholic priest giving a benediction. She performed this gesture as she backed slowly out of the room, at last shutting the door in front of her.

After a two-hour drive south from her place, she found herself chain smoking while parked in a quiet residential area of the Valley near where she had grown up. The familiarity was comforting, even though she hadn't felt like that belonged anywhere near there for almost a decade. Her parents had sold their house and retired out of state long ago, leaving their "freak" daughter behind to find her own way in the world. They had wanted a daughter they could show off and brag to their friends about. A nice, normal girl, with a nice, normal career.

"Going great, guys, thanks for asking." she said aloud to the empty street as she shakily lit another cigarette.

Meanwhile, her phone hadn't stopped filling up with messages. She had nowhere to go and was too scared to go home, where the shoes were likely still shedding volumes of darkened plasma, platelets, and red cells in her cabinet. She was also too scared of her friends and their sudden obsessiveness to try to visit any of them. No, she couldn't talk to them about this. Didn't want to feed them any more information that would keep fanning the flames of their joint interest in the shoes.

The notion that her friends' obsessiveness with the shoes and those shoes penchant for bleeding were somehow connected approached from the back of her mind, but the sheer terror that it implied she defensively kept at bay. She would have lost her grip had her conscious mind not done so.

She was still so tired. What if it had all been a dream? Did one of her friends slip something into her drink the last time they were out together? She'd never left their table, yet their hands had been everywhere. Always greedily returning to caress the shoes. She was so wound up with excitement over their attention, maybe she hadn't noticed a stray hand giving her cocktail a little boost. Percy would have thought of it as his little contribution to the night's fun. But still, for him to not ask and just do that was unacceptable, to say the least.

Fleeing to this once safe area was a waste of time. She had to go back to her apartment and check on the shoes. Maybe she was having a breakdown and it was all in her head. She had been under an immense amount of pressure to make ends meet. Being a freelance artist sounded romantic, but it was a constant hustle. Maybe Percy had given her something and she'd just had a terrible reaction.

These were sufficient rationalizations for her to regain the presence of mind to go back to her apartment. She sighed, started her car, and began the journey home. It was morning, and with traffic, it took three hours to get home instead of the two to get to her not-sanctuary. She arrived home at nine am, two mornings removed from the night out at the clubs

Acte Quatre.

The elevator doors opened on her floor, and there stood none other than Percy, lingering outside the front door to her flat in the hallway. Her apartment building had once been a grand hotel. Now, it was just another old, poorly maintained building populated by of a mix of struggling artists, lower income families, and retirees. Percy's ersatz bohemian attire allowed him to blend in as if he'd been a resident there all his life.

"Hey!" he called, waving to her. "Why aren't you answering my messages? Where have you been?"

She noticed that he was looking down at her worn Doc Martens and frowning.

"I just needed some air. Whatever you slipped me the other night really messed me up. Next time you do that, maybe give me a little warning, ok?"

When she drew near, she saw that Percy's face looked as if he'd spent the past twenty-four hours in hell. His eyes appeared heroin hollow. Clothes rumpled as if he'd been sleeping in them since last week. He was still in the same outfit from when they had gone to the club, but they looked as if they'd been worn for weeks, not a couple of days. She had never seen Percy like this and her fear, which had dissipated on the drive back home, was back again suddenly and completely.

"Wha- what? I didn't slip you anything. I wouldn't do something like that! Why would you even think that?" Percy looked genuinely hurt, and he was right to be. Percy could come across like a stuck-up brat even when he was at his most mature, but he wasn't the kind of asshole that she or any of her other friends couldn't trust with their safety. So why did she think that he'd dosed her?

Because she had wanted it to be true. The alternative meant that either the shoes were cursed, or she was losing her mind.

"I know. I'm sorry. It's been a rough day or two, alright? I really need more sleep and shit, Percy, you look like you do too. Talk later, ok? I promise I'll text you when I wake up." As she was talking to him, she slowly switched their positions, inching towards the door with her key in hand. His eyes weren't following her, fixed to a random point on the wall.

By the time he realized she had dismissed him… she had already opened her door, rushed in, and slammed it shut, throwing the deadbolt and door chain in place. She expected him to knock and demand to come in, but the hallway was silent. Whatever. She had work to do. She couldn't let the last few hours continue to distract her. The bills certainly wouldn't wait for her to sort her shit out. She booted up her computer, made a cup of tea and settled in. She had been working for only an hour when she realized that there was no trace of the tainted blood smell to be had anywhere. She'd been so preoccupied with ducking Percy she'd forgotten all about what she'd run from in the first place.

This development is good, is it not? Maybe it had been all just pure exhaustion, or perhaps something similar?

She asked herself these questions as she opened the bathroom door and braced herself for the onslaught. Nothing. She sniffed at the air trapped within as if there had been particles of coke suspended on each molecule of oxygen. Nothing again. Time, then, for the real test. Slowly, she opened the cabinet and peered at the plastic bag with the shoes. The bags looked clean. No bright red blood showing through. No dried brown-red smears either.

She sat down on the cold tile and ripped open the bags. There they were. Her beautiful shoes. Smelling like leather and looking as they had when she first purchased them. She checked for the first scuff that she had noticed the first night. Nothing. No unusual scent. She ran her hands over the clear rhinestones and ornate silver buckle.

"Oh," she huffed out in relief as she slowly caressed the shoes. "I'm so sorry, babies. I guess Momma hasn't been really feeling well. Throwing you on the floor like that, having buyer's remorse. Shame on me! I bet the others never feel that. They don't have to worry about surviving the way that I do. It's not your fault. Mommy's sorry."

Looking at the shoes, she experienced the feeling she had when she had seen them for the first time in the shop window.

"I'm glad I have you. Even if rent is going to be a little tougher to make this month."

Some people talk to their pets or plants. I guess I talk to my fancy shoes, she thought.

She felt as a breeze…

must by the time she'd finished working, washing up, and making herself ready for bed. She placed the shoes by her front door, pointed outwards so she could slip into them easily while grabbing her keys and purse. She had been so used to her boot occupying that rarified spot near the exit, but she wanted to wear the shoes out tomorrow. Go surprise Daphne and the others. Maybe they'd have finally gotten over her having just one thing that they all wanted and yet could never have. Then they could be onto their next new sparkly bauble, and their friendships could go back to how they were before.

"Let's give our public what they want, my dears, a show straight from the *Grand Guignol* of old, a show…spec-tac-u-lar!!!" she proclaimed to the shoes, laughing as she flipped off the lights and hopped into bed.

Sometime in the night, she woke, suddenly alert, a slow dread sweeping first from her head, then through her torso turning her insides to jelly as it moved to her legs and then feet. When that dread struck her toes, it had the effect of freezing her dead in place.

She blinked in the total darkness, eyes slowly adjusting to the pitch. The apartment's hall sconces were always on all night. She should have been able to see a light beneath the front door, but there was nothing.

Wait.

No.

There WAS something. A small flicker. She strained against the paralysis, managing to slowly roll sideways. Bracing herself on the bed rails, she leaned down to peer at the dark space in the door gap. At first, she saw nothing. But as her eyes continued to adjust, she saw that it was Percy standing there.

He was stretched out across the length of the door, one eye open and unblinking, staring fixedly at the spot where her shoes were sitting. In the dark, his one visible pupil was blown wide, a giant black bead. He looked like a starving rat. She could hear his strained breathing, a fast, low panting. He never looked over at her, only a few feet away in the tiny apartment, and she quickly pulled herself back up, wrapping her blankets around her and squeezing her eyes shut, desperate to fall back asleep and stop the trembling that wracked her body.

She awoke with a start to the familiar sound of her elderly neighbor's TV blasting. It sounded like he was marathoning *Law and Order* again. A moment later, the memory of Percy at her door like a demon junkie came back. Her eyes shot to the door. She could see the hallway beyond the gap easily in the day. Percy was gone.

She got out of bed, showered, dressed quickly, and checked her phone. The texts from Percy had stopped, and the others' texts had started to slow down as well. She shot a quick text to Daphne.

Hey. Sorry. I've been feeling really sick. Can I come over and hang for a bit?

Her phone dinged before she even had a chance to slip it back into her purse. *Mara and I are already on our way to come visit. See you soon.*

That was weird. Her friends had never come inside to her place, not even once, in the entire time they'd known each other. While they praised the building's architecture and history from the outside whenver they picked her up there, she knew that her apartment was too small and shabby for them to want to spend more than a few minutes inside.

Her phone dinged again as she slipped on her shoes and went to grab her keys. She probably had just enough time to run to the bodega and pick up a few drinks for them. She glanced down, expecting it to be Daphne again, but it was from her agent.

Good news. They've accepted your screenplay. We'll go over the details later. Meet tomorrow at 10AM?

She read it again and again, frozen to the spot before her door. Her grin grew broader and broader with each pass of the text. She did a little hop and heard the shoes tinkle like bells, the strap a little loose and the rhinestone chain making a lovely sound. "I finally did it! You're my lucky charms, my babies!" She stopped for a moment, reconsidered her last statement, and corrected herself.

"*We* did it."

She was still looking down at the shoes as she flicked the locks back. The door swung inward, striking her forehead squarely between the eyes and knocking her tumbling backwards. There was no opportunity to steady herself before something else ensured her journey to….

…the floor would be completed. The back of her skull struck the hardwood with a sickening crack. Her vision blurred, but she could still make out the tall, thin figure of Percy looming above her. He closed the door and flipped the deadbolt, not taking his eyes off her. No, not her. The shoes again. Always the shoes.

"Percy, wha—"

"Take them OFF, you fucking bitch! I NEED THEM!" he screamed, yanking her leg up abruptly and pulling on the shoe.

"Ow. Percy! Stop!" She yelled, trying to simultaneously pull her leg back and her dress down. She kicked at him uselessly. He was so much bigger than her and her head was still spinning from the fall. She was probably concussed.

"Why won't it come OFF," he yelled, still yanking. The chain was now scraping against the top of her foot, and she could see that she was bleeding.

"Percy stop, please!" she cried as he dragged her across the room, yanking all the while on the shoe, trying to remove it from her foot.

"You don't deserve to have something so great as these, you disgusting peasant."

For some reason, despite the absurdity and the sudden violence, that was the thing that finally snapped her into action. This wasn't Percy, was it? Sure, he was a spoiled rich kid but he had always seemed to accept people at face value.

Now she was a disgusting peasant? Was this what he had always actually thought of her? Was she just some kind of charity project to him? To all of them? A joke?

Little moments from over the years, previously ignored and dismissed, began to appear in her mind, like fireflies on a summer night. Knowing glances between the others. A smirk here. A scoff there. A quick turn away or a straightening of countenances when she glanced up to look. Looks and sounds that she was used to hearing from her family, from teachers. She always picked up on these signals too late, registering them in her memory, then wondering if they had simply been imagined. Why had she overlooked this behavior in her friends? Because she had wanted a home in this city of struggling artists and weirdos? A place with people like her, where she finally fit in?

But they weren't anything like her. She was still in her own world, on the outside. Percy had just confirmed that. She had always been alone.

She looked at him from her vantage point on the floor as he continued to fumble with the decorative buckle, yanking on her other foot to no avail. He was still in the same unwashed clothes, and his skin had a grayish cast to it. His eyes had that same black, beady, hungry rat look of the night before. For a moment, she felt tears well up for one of the first friends that she thought she had made in this lonely city.

The pity she felt was as fleeting as Percy's so-called friendship. It vanished.

Then she got angry.

Using her smaller body as leverage, she tucked her knees, pulling him forward and off balance. With her shoes planted on his torso, she used all the strength in her legs to flip him over and past her, as if they had rehearsed this maneuver as part of a gymnastics routine. She heard him collide with her writing desk. Before she could get to her feet and either scream or run or both, he was on her again, pulling her head back by her hair. They struggled on the floor, and she realized that he would kill her for her shoes. It was either her or him.

She heard her shoes tinkling again, prettily, as she and Percy continued to struggle. Her babies were afraid for mommy, and they wanted to help mommy…*to help her*…*KILL THE BAD MAN.*

"You want them so badly?" She screamed in his face, twisting to reach her foot, one hand holding his head back as one would with a wild animal biting at its prey.

"Have them, then!" she yelled as she slipped one of the shoes off and began to beat at his face with the heel. He didn't even scream or stop trying to grab at her as the heel punctured through one of his eyes. The socket exploded first in a geyser of blood, tissue, and the aqueous humor of the eye, but after just four direct blows to the socket, she had struck oil in the form of bits of Percy's frontal cortex.

She kept bashing, now sitting astride him and bringing the shoe down over and over again. She felt his nose crack and a spray of blood…

…shoot up at her. Somehow, he continued to try to grab at the shoe, not to fend it off, but to stroke it. All while his other hand continued trying to choke her. She kept bringing the shoe down until he finally stopped moving. She looked down at the once beautiful face of her friend, now a bloody, unrecognizable pulp of tissue and bone fragments.

All was finally quiet in the apartment. She heard the neighbor's TV blasting the end of a commercial, followed by the sound of the *Law and Order* gavel.

She rolled off Percy and looked down at the shoe still on her right foot. She watched in fascination as tiny tendrils of blood started to split off from the larger pool that had formed. She blinked as the droplets joined together, and eventually a steady stream of blood began inching towards the shoe.

She didn't scream. Only watched.

This is shock. I'm in shock, she thought.

The liquid swirled around the shoes, creating a gorgeous and delicate vortex. The blood began to crawl upward, slowly covering them. She watched as both shoes remade themselves while the floor slowly cleared of any blood that remained, like it was being slurped up as a root beer float through a straw. One by one, the clear stones slowly turned red. She stared into the crystals as they sparkled, the blood swaying hypnotically as each one filled up.

By the time Daphne and Mara arrived fifteen minutes later, she was prepared. She was dressed to go out, the now bright, shining, cherry red leather and garnet shoes on her feet, one hand behind her back.

"Come in! We're gonna have a shoe try-on party in a minute," she announced as she flung the door open.

Both women looked stunned, but hastily walked in as she shut the door behind them. She saw them this time as they happened - the whispering and the laughing and the talking - and not in the mind's eye of memory weeks later. Mara whispered something to Daphne and Daphne glanced back and snickered.

Daphne didn't even have time to turn fully around. The kitchen knife went in cleanly between the vertebrae of her exposed neck and she went down instantly, eyes wid eand body convulsing. Mara made it even easier. She opened her mouth as if to scream, but in fact an invitation.

"You make it all so easy," she said as she buried the knife in Mara's mouth, pulling it out sideways, splitting her cheek in half.

The meeting the next morning went better than she had hoped. She'd received a generous payout just for signing on the bottom line. She would not only be able to be comfortable, but maybe even a little well off for the first time in her life. They wanted her next three scripts, as well. Her agent, smelling money like Percy likely had smelled her shoes, informed the studio that they'd get back to them, to re-negotiate. Re-negotiate! Ha!

On their way out, her agent glanced down at her shoes. She felt herself stiffen a bit with tension. She only just smiled and went back to looking at her paperwork, almost absently commenting, "Those are lovely."

"You…you don't want them yourself?" she asked.

"Oh no, hon. But I do *love* my new earrings," her agent flicked at her left ear, and exchanged a knowing glance with her client. "But those my dear, those…suit you."

"Thank you. They do, don't they?" and the shoes gave a little reassuring tinkle. The time would come, in this city where friends were few, and enemies were many. She'd have to decide who were the ones that would do her harm. But she smiled because in the end, she knew the shoes would help her choose.

THEATRE DU

GRAND GUIGNOL

20 bis rue CHAPTAL TÉL.TRI.28·34 M° BLANCHE PIGALLE

LE BAISER DE MINUIT

Drame En 5 actes - Directeur wp Quigley

MllMAXA-MM.GOUGET.ORVALLERICHE, DE NEVRY, ETC

Acte Un.

"Will you fucking COME ON?!?" the girl in the skimpy crimson dress half-asked, half-screamed at the closed and locked bathroom door. The girl then began to pound her fist on that door, hard enough to rattle the doorknob. She then added at a much lower, almost whispered volume:

"I'm not having your gross leaky ass problems fuck-up my New Years, PJ, now *let's…go.*"

Inside the bathroom, simultaneously clutching his midsection and regretting his recent life decisions, the boy with his jeans around his ankles muttered to himself in the muted volume of a person in digestive agony.

"Well Sandra, maybe if you didn't have to insist on a gluten, meat, and taste-free meal every fucking night I wouldn't have had to f-"

At that very second, a soldering iron of pain stabbed at the spot in his belly where his lower intestine theoretically began.

"Feel…."

Another stab in the exact same spot.

"Like…."

A third stab, only this time, it struck in the center of his abdomen, just above the base of his dick.

This followed by a volley of Sandra's fists on the bathroom door.

"Let's go…P-"she did not get to the J before he could take no more.

"I'M FUCKING DYING IN HERE, SANDRA!!!!"

Minutes later, in the car:

Save for the sound of Sandra's heater at its maximum setting, blasting warmed and recycled and gasoline-tainted air into the front seat of the Camry, the car ride was silent.

For the first twenty minutes, anyway.

Devoid of even the slightest bit of conversation, PJ, was who not used to riding shotgun while his girlfriend drove, managed to curb the urge to continually monitor her driving and glanced over at his way-too-fucking-significant other but once. And only for a second.

He just needed to confirm that Sandra had already contorted her features into the grotesque amalgamation of equal parts anger, disgust, revulsion, and regret he referred to as her…. patented "Diaperface" expression. Indeed, Diaperface was in fact present and accounted for the journey to this party that Diaperf…*Sandra* was all fuckin' up-in-arms about arriving to on time.

PJ glumly looked out of the passenger side window and sunk his chin into an open palm. He watched the dimly lit streets and barren trees roll by. He thought to himself:

Why the fuck didn't I just leave years ago?

Why didn't she just leave?

Why did it all have to come to this bullshit?

PJ and Sandra approached a stoplight. As if directed by some prankster element of the cosmos, the light turned yellow, and then red mere seconds before Sandra could get there. She was forced to stop. She pursed her lips into an O-shape and let out an aggravated puff of air. PJ didn't look, but when he heard the sound she'd made with her forced exhale, the image of Sandra's lips as an actual butthole letting out a fragrance-free fart popped into his head.

This relationship just had to end. It *needed* to end.

Sandra brought the Camry to a stop at the stupid fucking stoplight that had just turned red. It was stupid and fucking because there wasn't another vehicle to be seen in any direction, and nor would there because they were out in the middle of nowhere. Sandra was stressed, because she was now certain that she wasn't going to get to the party with enough time to retrieve her specially chosen *cotillon.*

Sandra's frustration ramped up with each successive motionless second, her hatred of the man sitting next to her following a similar trend. She thought of PJ's face. He'd be sitting there with that dull, unaffected look, not concerned even in the slightest bit how important getting to this party on time was for her. PJ never cared a single bit about what was important to her for the entire time they'd been together – their finances, their social standing, even their sex life. PJ hadn't touched her or even made a move on her in months. She had needs, and PJ met none of them. She took a deep breath in through her nose, and forcefully pushed it out through her mouth.

The last straw had been a couple of months ago, when one night she'd gone out and bought a cheerleader's outfit to greet PJ…

…in their bedroom to try and entice him. The thing looked fucking ridiculous, and she hated wearing it from the second she put it on. Nonetheless, she sprawled herself out on their bed and waited for him to come home. PJ came through the front door, then through the bedroom door. He looked at Sandra, and all the fucker could do was ask why she was dressed like a cheerleader. He put his carry-all down on the ground at the foot of the bed and went back out to the living room to watch football. She'd never been so embarrassed for herself in her entire life.

This relationship had to end. It *needed* to end. And she was going to end it.

The light had still not turned green, and Sandra's frustration had reached its breaking point. *Fuck this,* she thought and..

PJ could feel Sandra getting ready to run the red light.

"Don't you fucking dare, Sandra. There could be a cop hiding…"

…she hit the gas pedal, peeling out of the four-way stoplight like a woman on a mission. PJ doing his wet blanket routine the second before she dropped the hammer only made her traffic transgression that much sweeter and satisfying in its release. Her frustration evaporated in an instant, and she could feel herself smiling in triumph.

"…in the trees," finished PJ He looked over at her and saw that she was then grinning from ear to ear. He snapped the heater off. She snapped it back on.

And then it was off to the races. Sandra and PJ bickered and argued the entire remainder of the car ride to Seth's house. Their respective speaking volumes started at indoor levels. Over the course of the ensuing twenty minutes, the intensity of their argument and commensurate decibel level rose so that by the time they'd made the turn onto the long dirt path that led to their destination, PJ and Sandra were straight screaming into each other's faces.

It had to end.

Acte Deux.

Seth and Jonathan were standing outside by the enormous front double doors to Seth's mansion. In the dark and in the distance, they both happened to notice a lone set of headlights slow down as they approached….

…the turn-off from the main road. Prior to the car bearing those headlights making the turn, PJ and Sandra's screaming had grown so loud Seth and Jonathan could not only hear them yelling from they stood, but also were able to discern the identity of the people in the vehicle.

"Hunh. The last to arrive. Sandra and PJ," Seth turned one side of his mouth up in a wry grin. "Talk about theatre."

Tonight was most certainly meant to be, Seth thought, and this most recent development was as clear a sign as any. He and Jonathan watched as Sandra and PJ pulled onto the half-mile long car track that carved through the surrounding woods to Seth's driveway, then down that path, finally coming to a stop at the far edge of the paved portion of said driveway.

Jonathan handed Seth a tiny glass jar and metal spoon when the car first turned onto the path. Seth wasted no time in digging a generous lump of coke out of the jar with the implement, then snapping the crystalline powder up into his one remaining functional nostril. While Seth performed this ritual Jonathan continued yapping away, as he'd been doing since they started in on the blow an hour before. Seth asked himself why he shared his drugs with Jonathan in the first place, as dipshit flapped his gums away.

"Hey man – is that? That? Is that Sandra Stetson and PJ Quinn? Dude, why would you even let these two participate in the festivities? I mean, doesn't this complicate shit a little more than it already is? Should we do something Seth? Hunh?"

"No, Jonathan. It's fine. I knew they were coming."

Jonathan turned from watching Sandra and PJ come up the driveway, took a step towards Seth so that his face was mere inches away from his snortin' buddies' face. Jonathan lowered his voice to creepy weirdo level as he did so for effect.

"Are you sure, brother? I mean, I know you got the history with Sandra and all that, but you and PJ…"

Seth pocketed the jar and the spoon as the car pulled closer. He then grasped Jonathan by the shoulder and gave Jonathan a firm but not violent shove backwards.

"Do you mind, bro? Jesus you always get so fuckin weird when you do coke. Take…

…it down. Like, immediately."

"I'm sorry Seth. No for real. I'm sorry. Okay?"

"Okay! Fuck. It's all good. They're on the list."'

"But I'm still one of the V.I.P's, right Seth?"

"*Jesus fucking Christ, Jonathan, yes.*"

Sandra and PJ's car found the last remaining spot at the far edge of the driveway. When the engine was shut off, so too was the shouting of both the passengers of the automobile. Sandra and PJ stepped out of the car and approached the house.

"Go inside and enjoy yourself Jonathan, and don't act like a fucking psychopath. I'll greet these two."

'But Seth I…"

"Dude, if I have to say one more thing to you, I'm gonna fucking kill Miss Kathy *and* you tonight. I have no problem whatsoever with one extra murder.

"But didn't you already…do…that?"

"There's still plenty of gas in my fucking chainsaw, shitstain. GO."

Jonathan looked positively hurt – and frightened. Without another peep, he sulked back inside. Seth pushed the door closed to ensure his removal from the situation and centered himself. Hearing the two sets of footsteps approaching from behind him on the stone walkway, he dispelled his annoyance with Jonathan and put on his game face. Tonight, that game face was the gracious, warm, debonair host to "the" New Year's Eve party of 2023.

He turned to greet the final two invitees to arrive. He extended his arms to embrace Sandra.

"The champagne has arrived!" he exclaimed.

Sandra's face brightened, and she quickened her pace to return Seth's embrace. She trotted up the broad, granite front steps and leapt into the man's arms.

"Seth McMillin, it has been too long," she gushed as she wrapped her arms around him as if she intended to never let him go for the remainder of the evening

PJ stood in the walkway, not even taking the first of the front steps, standing still and regarding the entire exchange with a look of disgust mixed with shame. This man…

…this Seth McMillin, was the same one who'd left her and sent her packing as it were, mere minutes after she'd informed him years before that she was pregnant with their child. Sandra had no choice but to have the abortion, especially considering that the child's father and the father's family had endless legal and financial resources at their disposal to ensure that Sandra would raise the child well and truly on her own.

Seth glanced past Sandra to PJ standing there and smiled at him.

"And this must be the famous PJ I keep hearing about," Seth said as he wriggled his way out from Sandra's Boa Constrictor-like grasp to greet his last guest. "Well don't be shy, PJ, come on up. It's so good to finally have you here. How we've waited!"

Sandra turned to watch Seth as he made to greet PJ and thought to herself, *how we've waited? Who's we?*

Seth extended his arms in the same welcoming gesture he had for Sandra, from which PJ recoiled. PJ extended his right hand instead for a standard handshake.

"Yeah, hey. I'm PJ," he said.

Seth dropped his arms and smiled at PJ.

"Of course. Apologies if I'm a little too friendly sometimes. Just how I am I guess," The two exchanged the more formalized greeting.

At that moment, PJ felt the same sharp pain in his abdomen as he had experienced just before he and Sandra had left for the party. Unable to hide it or shake it off, PJ grabbed at his stomach with both arms. He made an anguished moaning sound.

"Oh jeez, PJ, are you okay man?"

"Y-yeah, just stomach problems, that's all."

From the top of the steps, Sandra took the opportunity to clarify the nature of PJ's intestinal distress.

"He's had diarrhea all night, Seth. We almost didn't make it, but I made sure we came!" Sandra blurted out, pleased as punch to reveal the embarrassing truth about PJ's current digestive issues, as well as the fact she'd made sure they showed up that evening.

Seth frowned a bit, turning his head to the side to acknowledge her exclamation.

"Well, hey man. Let's get you inside. Maybe a drink or two will help calm your plumbing down."

PJ merely looked up at Seth as if to say, 'are you fucking crazy dude?'

Seth saw this and stumbled through the last part of his reassurance.

"We've got everything, so I'm sure we can find you something that'll work."

"Yeah, sure, whatever man. Let's just get inside," replied PJ.

PJ meandered forward, Seth walking alongside his ailing guest. They climbed the steps, joining Sandra. The three of them entered Seth's house proper.

The interior of Seth McMillin's house was extravagant, magnificent, breathtaking, and stunning, all at once. From the high, vaulted ceilings, to the polished marble flooring in the apartment-sized dining area and sitting room, from the mahogany bookcases stocked with first editions, plush hand-crafted European furniture in that same sitting room to the long oak table back in the dining area, every aspect of Seth's residence spoke of affluence and of privilege.

"Sandra, PJ, the coat room is just in front of you." Seth pointed directly ahead of them to a door, slightly ajar. Sandra stepped ahead and pulled it open, beyond which was a room larger than most people's bedrooms - room enough for about sixty or seventy of the room's namesake pieces of winter apparel to reside in.

"Seth, this…this is your coat room?" asked Sandra, in a voice so inflected that it marked her as the first woman in history that became horny at just the sight of such a space.

"Yes, my dear Dom Perignon," Seth gently grasped her by the elbow. Without taking his gaze from upon her eyes, Seth called over his shoulder.

"PJ, are you going to drop off your coat?"

PJ, for his part, looked whiter than a Kenny Chesney concert - not that Sandra or Seth would have noticed at that moment.

"I'm…I'm going to keep my coat on. I'm freezing. D-don't feel well."

Sandra elbowed Seth and rolled her eyes. PJ saw this and frowned.

"Sandra, you mustn't be too hard on him. Now come, let's join the others," Seth said.

The three of them made off down the hallway to the left to make their way to the ballroom proper, Seth and Sandra gliding down the hall like prom dates while PJ trailed behind like an ersatz Quasimodo. As they strolled down that stretch of the manse, PJ took notice that while one side was lined with black and alabaster baroque statues, and the other with intricately paneled windows to one side. But more than their immediate surroundings, he also took note that Sandra and Seth's voices could be heard echoing down the hall.

"And where is Miss Kathy, Seth? I'd think she'd be down here with you, greeting guests, shaking hands, and making merry."

"No, I'm afraid Kathy will not be joining us this evening in the ballroom. She said she was much too tired for the festivities, so we shared our midnight kiss before anyone arrived."

Upon hearing that, Sandra drew so close to Seth that no discernible empty space could be seen between them.

"You don't say…" replied Sandra.

Directly above that first-floor hallway was one directly above it on the second floor of Seth's lavish abode. The inner walls that defined both comprised one load-bearing structure, so that if the house had been completely silent, anyone standing on the second floor could easily hear any conversations in the hallway below. This was not the case, however, as Rick and Erin Puth, a married couple of eleven years were upstairs, engaged in a bitter exchange over, of all things, who's turn it had been to remain sober that evening to drive home. They had stepped away from the ballroom to hold their argument in private.

"I can't believe this, Rick. We both agreed last fucking night that I could enjoy myself tonight and have whatever drinks I wanted, and you'd drive home."

"You know that never happened Erin. You always pull your gaslighting shit whenever we have a night out, so you can make me feel bad about ruining your night. Every fucking time. We never had that conversation." Rick absently played with the switchblade he held in his trousers pocket.

"Or maybe you were too high to remember, *Rick*. I thought that I smelled-"

At that moment, Rick removed his hand from his pants and placed it on his wife's shoulder to stop her mid-admonishment.

"Hey. Wait. Do you smell that?" Rick grimaced, his sense of smell detecting…

something strange nearby.

"What, Rick. Somebody smoking *weed*," she chided.

Rick gave her a look as if to say, 'obviously not, douchebag', to which Erin stopped. Erin then detected the aroma too.

She sniffed at the air like a bloodhound. "Smells like…gasoline?"

Rick agreed. "Yep. No doubt. Gasoline." The couple followed the pungent odor to the closed door of what was likely a bedroom. Rick tried the door, but it was locked shut.

"Hunh. Might be Seth's room. Who knows what kind of kinky shit he's got going on in there?"

Erin smacked Rick on the shoulder, a can-you-please-behave blow.

"C'mon. Let's just go back downstairs. You can sober up in the next couple of…"

"The fuck I am, Erin,"

And with that, the Puths returned downstairs.

Behind the door, which indeed led to Seth's bedroom, a recently used chainsaw sat on the ground just a few feet from the door. There were bits of flesh, a splinter or two of pulverized bone caught in the chain's teeth, and the entire blade was covered in the brownish red of blood almost completely coagulated from a few hours previous.

Over on Seth's bed, were the remains of 'Miss Kathy'. Seth had kept the chainsaw just under her side of the bed so that he'd be able to pull the thing started, bring it down onto her neck to decapitate her before she could react. This strategy half-worked - Kathy was able to move her head to the side just a few inches before Seth had made his killing stroke. The result was a cut that ran through her teeth, her mouth agape as it struck, one far messier had it instead run through her neck as was planned. This slight alteration pleased Seth, and with absolute fervor ground her face and jaw all the way down until he did manage to separate most of her head from her body. A partial decapitation proved more satisfying than a full one, it seemed.

Seth didn't stop there, however, and severed her arms and legs with her corpse in place, so that…

…when the chainsaw finally ceased its mechanical braying, Miss Kathy resembled a Barbie doll that hadn't yet been assembled from its constituent parts. When he'd finished, Seth placed the saw on the ground and gave Kathy a peck on her mangled cheek.

"Happy New Year, darling."

Acte Trois.

At the other end of the museum-like hallway Sandra, Seth, and PJ had just traversed was one of the first-floor kitchens. This was a pedestrian affair compared to the rooms that had come before, with nothing extravagant about the cabinets, counters, and serving island within it. Even the eight or nine partygoers present in area were less than impressive - some leaned against a counter staring blankly into space, while others stood by themselves with arms folded and faces painted different shades of terminally irritated or terminally bored. It was silent in that kitchen, except for a low conversation between two plain looking women talking about serrated knives for some reason.

Sandra stopped in the middle of the kitchen's open area, anticipating Seth doing the same, to begin making all the introductions to the people that would be part of her new life with him. She scanned the room, eyes bouncing from each disaffected person to the next, brimming with anticipation of hearing about whatever charmed lives they all led.

Instead, Seth only slowed for a moment and nudged her forward.

"Step lively my little champagne, the real party is through here in the ballroom."

Sandra, despite feeling off-put at Seth's rushing her through, giggled nonetheless at the sound of her new pet name. And did he just say…a ballroom? An actual ballroom? All PJ could ever afford for the two of them was a shitty two-bedroom apartment. She'd been forced to endure this untenable condition of living for years. Yes, it was fine for a while, but when it was clear they'd be locked in for life into this middle-class existence, Sandra began looking for an out. As they continued on their journey, PJ lumbering behind them like a pack mule, Sandra concluded that most of the people in that room were mostly if not all 'plus ones', the poor fools.

Maybe PJ should stay in here with the other future corpses, thought Sandra…

"That the bathroom, Seth?" PJ asked.

"You know it is, my man!" Seth "Cool, just making sure I knew where it was in case I…'

"In case you have to take a gross shit, PJ?" Sandra asked in the most revolted voice she could manage.

"Yes, dear," PJ confirmed.

After passing through one final room, a study that was defined by towering mahogany bookcases set against all four walls and a leather sitting chair, Seth, Sandra, and PJ were finally upon the ballroom.

It opened before them, and Sandra audibly gasped at the sight of it.

To match his better half's gasp, PJ let out an audible fart - one loud enough to be heard over the gathered party goers, music, and general noise of the room.

Of course, he has to ruin the moment, thought Sandra.

Disgusting.

She couldn't bear to turn around to face PJ, to acknowledge her struggling boyfriend.

From behind Sandra and Seth, PJ squeaked:

"Guys, I'm just gonna see myself to the bathroom, don't think I'm gonna make it much further. Excuse me."

Seth turned to PJ and smiled at him.

"O.K. big guy. Do what you need to do. We'll be ready when you're ready, bud."

PJ smiled back at him and meandered back to the bathroom off of the kitchen they'd just strolled through.

Sandra put PJ out of her mind and to take in the ballroom before her. It was truly magnificent.

To the left was a buffet table, a long, black piece made of darkened pine and coated with a glowing, exquisite finish. It ran the entire length of the wall, which was at least fifty feet. Positioned on a pedestal was an ice sculpture, intricately carved into the shape of Janus, the two-faced Roman god of gates and calendars.

One face looked friendly and wise, the other sinister, menacing, and corrupt.

The ballroom floor was polished marble, cut into a hypnotic pattern of geometric shapes - triangles, squares, hexagons, and octagons set into the surface at regular intervals.

Above, three gold and glass chandeliers that glowed with hundreds of warm yellow bulbs provided the ambiance and lighting. Music played from seemingly everywhere at once - a slow waltz that sounded as if lifted right from the soundtrack to *The Great Gatsby*.

The ballroom was a hundred feet long by its far wall, which was marked with intermittent sets of glass double doors that led out onto an expansive back veranda. The doors had been locked for the evening however, and no partygoers were outside.

Those in attendance were all dressed to the nines – without exception. The men were sharp and smart, the women radiant and elegant. Sandra then looked to her right and took notice of the last defining characteristic of the ballroom.

Set about ten feet from the ground and built as an extension into the ballroom from the remainder of the second floor was a small balcony. It looked like one that the leader of a third-world country, or possibly the Pope might appear upon to greet and address his people or flock.

Sandra nodded to it and nudged Seth.

"That where you're planning on watching the proceedings?" she asked.

"*Mais oui,* my sweet little bubbly. Your *cotillon*, I believe a...meat cleaver, is in a box in the side room. You have your instructions, dear."

"I do, Seth. Oh, I can't wait to get on with our new life, dear."

"Nor can I."

Just then a strange, bearded man named Vernon approached and introduced himself to Sandra.

"You must be Seth's champagne…Sandra, isn't it?"

Sandra again giggled at her nickname.

"Yes, thank you. And you are?" The man curtly introduced himself, and then glared at Seth.

"Excuse me, dear, I must be off. I'll join you soon enough."

Sandra watched as the two of them walked off.

Sandra checked the time.

It was eleven-fifteen.

She went to retrieve her cleaver surreptitiously, and then at last joined the party in full.

It was ten minutes to midnight. By then, PJ had been in that goddamned bathroom for over a half-hour, but it wasn't as if Sandra minded or even remotely cared until that point. She'd spent that time bouncing from person to person, attempting to discern whether the individual she spoke to was one of the 'plus ones' or one of the 'invited'. She felt as though she had a pretty good grasp of who was who but was careful not to hint at the true nature of the party.

It had been styled as the time and the event for new beginnings, a clean slate for the couples in attendance and Seth had provided the opportunity for all to do it in class and style. This was the first prerequisite to have been invited to that mansion, that monument to refinement and elegance for that New Years' Eve – only those people in committed relationships were bid to come to the gala that night.

Seth's invitation bore a second prerequisite.

There were times when one party in a relationship wanted more than just to move into the future onto the shore on the other side of the bridge as themselves, a solo act, and leave their partner behind. They desired to not just burn that bridge down but blow it the fuck up. And in this day and age, with the rules and laws of normative society restricting one's ability to do just that, there never seemed to be a chance to do so.

Until Seth had sent his invitations back in November, and Sandra had received hers.

Sandra wandered over to the buffet table after having her fill of socializing with some of the guests. There was a subdued feeling shared by almost everyone with whom she spoke. This was no surprise, however, seeing as how it was likely that everyone there was in one state of abject misery or another.

At once, Seth appeared on the balcony at the opposite end of the ballroom, accompanied by Vernon and a woman – Shannon, whom she'd just met in her recent travels. There were two other individuals that joined them on the precipice, and together those that joined Seth bore a strange look of concern at the gathered masses. Sandra surmised they were there in case there was any 'cleaning up' to do, which was a possibility

There was so much that could go wrong. Someone might get cold feet, one of the 'plus ones' may get the better of their partner. How many were here? Forty, fifty, even sixty people? That likely meant that thirty people were about to -

Seth took a microphone into his hand from a stand placed on his left. The music quieted, the crowd hushed, and waited for their host to speak. Seth addressed the party.

"Good evening my friends and thank you all so much for coming to the first 'Midnight Kiss' New Year's Eve Gala!"

A round of applause came from sixty-six people present, although it was hardly rousing, hardly enthusiastic. One would be forgiven for thinking that it the clapping seemed perfunctory and pained.

"As we approach the New Year, all of us gathered are here to celebrate not just a time of new beginnings, but the loved ones we'll be making our new beginnings with!"

More weak clapping.

"Both myself and my closest friends here with me," Seth continued, motioning to his four lackeys, "will watch your passionate exchanges with hope, happiness, and admiration as our gathered couples engage in a midnight kiss to commemorate this auspicious occasion!"

A third round of weak clapping.

Seth didn't seem to notice, nor care. He blew a kiss to the crowd, as if he were bidding a 'Dating Game' audience goodnight at the conclusion of an exceptionally awkward episode. He set the microphone down and began conversing to Shannon, who'd taken up position just next to him. He appeared panicked for a moment and picked the microphone up again.

"And don't forget - our VIP guests will be gathering just after midnight in the downstairs games room for our special presentation!"

Eight or nine people standing in the ball room took notice of this – including Jonathan. Jonathan's jaw slid back and forth as a typewriter would, signaling to everyone he was at least eight ball deep at that moment. Those individuals let loose with a bizarrely enthusiastic series of whoops and cheers.

Sandra again took notice of the clock. Five minutes until midnight, and it was then that panic swept through her and the crimson dress she wore, down her matching heels.

PJ was still nowhere to be found. Sandra thought:

Holy shit. He's still in the fucking john.

She finished the tuna tartar appetizer she'd been absently munching upon. She quickly checked her back slip for her *cotillon* to see that it was secure. In doing so, she caught sight of an odd yet striking short-haired girl molesting the shrimp cocktail, rather than taking one and moving on. She was filling an oversized Ziploc bag with the waste.

"Ughhh," shew said aloud to her.

The short-haired girl glared back at Sandra.

"Go fuck yourself, cunt."

Sandra took that prompt as one good as any to go hunt down PJ.

Three minutes until midnight.

Sandra stood alone in the now empty kitchen. The stragglers that had been present when they'd first arrived had moved to the ballroom long before. She knocked on the door.

"PJ, hon, it's time for the midnight kiss. Are you almost done?"

"Yeah, almost. Out in a few minutes."

"Sweetheart, you need to come out…*now*."

Sandra's anxiety, already pinned, elevated into a realm of alarm she'd never felt in her life.

What would Seth think?

Moreover, what would he do if she didn't complete her kiss?

Would he be mad? Would he…

She pushed the thought from her mind. There was too much at stake. Sandra left the knock behind and found herself banging on a bathroom door yet again that evening.

"Hon, you need to come out now. Please!"

"I said I'll be out in a fucking minute, Sandra!"

One minute.

Thirty seconds.

Sandra frantically beat her fist in a frantic, desperate drumbeat against Seth's bathroom door. Although she was careful, the cleaver began to slip out of its place in her dress and… down her hip.

down her hip.

It was no use. She yanked the cleaver out and held it her right hand at the ready for the second PJ opened the door.

"SWEETHEART PLEASE!!!! WE'RE GOING TO MISS OUR KISS! MIDNIGHT!!!"

Sandra stopped banging on the door when she heard everyone out in the dining and living room area, gathered by twos, with each couple spending their last seconds together before the scheduled massacre would ensue. All counted down the seconds in unison until the big moment.

The sixty-six partygoers chanted: "FIVE…FOUR…THREE…TWO…"

Acte Final

"ONE!!"

Adam Kinzinger leaned into his wife Barbara; his lips puckered. Barbara plunged a thick piece of sharpened wood that looked suitable for Nosferatu up and into the meaty part of Adam's jaw. Barbara had balked the day before about going through it, but earlier that evening, when she saw Adam grab a generous handful of Jaime Card's ass, the reticence vanished. Barbara had noted Jaime's position in the seconds before midnight, hoping she was one of the 'plus ones'. Joyfully, Barbara saw her husband decapitating her with a pair of hedge clippers. Where that man had kept them was a mystery Barbara hoped to solve a bit later. What storage space that man must have!

Meanwhile, Adam's alcohol-soaked eyes shot open the instant the point breached his jaw and broke through his lower palate. He attempted to cry out, but the location and trajectory of Barbara's thrust rendered him unable to speak. Blood poured from his neck like runny tomato soup from a pot, and Barbara turned her gaze back to him only to mouth the words "happy new year" to him. He fell to his knees, and then to the ground. He fell face first into a puddle of roughly two liters of his soup-blood had already accumulated.

The clock had struck midnight.

And so, it had begun.

Knives, cleavers, hammers, appeared from nowhere and everywhere. They were drawn from behind backs and under clothes, from dress jacket pockets and from spots secured under dresses and gowns.

There was an outlier to those more conventional tools, in which a large, thick cellophane Ziploc bag spotted at the party earlier, had made its reappearance. The young woman who chosen to roll to her own punk "Death by Ziploc" tune, Autumn Zabriski, had been filling said bag with cocktail sauce and discarded shrimp shells since eleven. That short-haired scary girl that had told Sandra to fuck off minutes before produced the convenient storage product from underneath her blouse. With one dexterous, nimble motion, she opened the bag's contents out onto the top of her girlfriend's head, blinding her. Autumn then pulled the bag down, yanked it tight around her partner's head, and asphyxiated the girl while at the same time the discarded shrimp remnants kicked off her victim's extreme allergy to shellfish. Overkill was not in Autumn Zabriski's dictionary.

Thirty-three couples had attended Seth's party, and thus thirty-three executions were carried out - the overwhelming majority carried out with bladed or pointed weapons. Firearms had been forbidden, for obvious reasons. Those with blades mostly struck at their mates at the neck area, attacks intended to render their victims helpless to scream and assure their demise. The visible result of this widely adopted strategy was the transformation of that gorgeous marble floor into Jackson Pollack rendered in just color – the bright ruby of oxygenated blood once headed towards roughly twenty or so people's brains.

Speaking of brains, the nine bludgeoning deaths were not as elegant, measured, or quick – but what they lacked in style was more than made up for in sheer savagery. Bob Sakamoto, armed with only a Billy club, first came across his wife Karen Sakamato' temple with the business end. The blow knocked her unconscious, and Karen dropped to the floor on her left side, in the same direction as Bob's blow. On Halloween, Karen had disclosed to Bob that she was a month pregnant with another man's child and that she'd already filed for divorce. Bob accepted the invitation within three minutes of receiving it, without checking with Karen to see if she'd even still go with him. After quite a bit of cajoling and coaxing, she relented and agreed to go - he'd sold it as just one last night out together after thirteen years of marriage. Bob flipped her onto her back.

Bob spent the first ten minutes of the New Year beating her abdomen with his Prohibition-era *cotillon*, never breaking through the flesh but rupturing almost every internal organ one could think of.

Marjorie Ocasio used a cast-iron meat tenderizer. She'd specifically selected it to forever silence the complaining her diminutive and terminally loudmouth husband Daniel did about her cooking, her looks, and how well she'd given him head over the years. The man never cooked a day in his life, rarely cleaned himself up or wore anything other than a tee-shirt and sweatpants, and *never* went down on her once in their twenty-four-year stint together. Marjorie had previously asked Seth permission if she could remove a few prime cuts from his corpse and wrap them up to take it with her at the end of the evening – a Daniel Doggie Bag.

Seth replied with a smiley emoji, followed by some words of encouragement:

"Let me know how he tastes!"

Thirty-three homicides.

Completed in just under three minutes.

The amount of blood spilled onto the ballroom floor was staggering. Seth and his cronies stood and watched. At the conclusion, the five of them sang in chorus together:

Should old acquaintance be forgot….

Three of the invitees vomited. A couple of them began to cry. Still a couple more began to giggle, then laugh outright. By the time the twisted rendition of "Auld Lang Syne" finished, there was silence.

Seth, Vernon, Shannon, Mac and Wednesday surveyed the carnage from their perch and saw that it was good.

The "midnight kiss" had gone off without so much as a single hitch, with none of the 'plus ones' putting up any real resistance. Shannon's buddy Autumn, with her sack of shrimp cocktail strangulation, by far provided the most entertaining and amusing kill. Shannon quickly pointed her out to the boys, who pointed and laughed the entire time Autumn savagely asphyxiated her companion. Autumn was the last one to finish, and when she had, she looked up at her audience.

Seth leaned over to Shannon.

"Autumn isn't on our VIP list, is she?"

Shannon shook her head violently.

"Fuck no, Seth. I like her. She's hilarious."

"Introduce us later, will ya? I like the cut of that girl's jib. MVP right there."

Just then, the evening's LVP appeared behind the group, looking as if he'd done enough coke to kill an elephant on the way up the stairs to the second floor alone.

"Ah hey guys. Looks like everything's done! What's up with the VIP gathering?" Jonathan asked.

Seth looked to the rest of his inner circle, nodding as he did so.

"Well bud, seeing as how you're right fucking on top of it, can you round the group up and bring them down to the games room in the basement?"

"Sure, Seth, will do! Oh man, I can't wait for this!" Jonathan disappeared.

Wednesday was confused.

"VIP gathering? What the hell is…"

Mac interrupted him.

"Dude, you didn't think that cops wouldn't figure out the people that survived were *exactly* one-half of the couples that showed up for the party?"

"Well, yeah, but…"

Seth stepped between Wednesday and Mac.

"Yeah, but nothing. Mac you know what to do. Wednesday go with him – and sorry I didn't tell you about this part. I'll save you both a glass of champagne."

Mac nodded. He placed his hand over his heart and looked upwards in a dramatic pose.

"My only regret is that I won't get to see that cork pop."

Seth and Mac laughed.

Seth regarded his remaining troops, Shannon and Vernon.

"Well, kids. Shall we?"

Vernon agreed.

"We most certainly fucking shall."

Moments later, Seth, Shannon, and Vernon arrived in the kitchen. They found Sandra sitting in chair, crying and nervously drinking a Mimosa. Vernon and Shannon, who had been carrying two or three champagne glasses in each hand, set them down on the kitchen island and helped Sandra to her feet.

"Why Sandra, what's the matter?"

"Oh, Seth. I'm so so sorry…" Sandra embraced Seth, cleaver in her left hand.

"I've been banging on that fucking door for twenty minutes, and the fucker still won't come out. I tried so…"

Seth smiled, and gently pushed her back by her shoulders.

"There there, my little *Dom Perignon*. I'll just unlock the door, and you can take care of business."

"You're - you're not mad?"

"Why no darling, of course not!" Seth took her hand in his and led her to the bathroom door. "Now, are you ready? I do believe this is the highlight of the evening."

Seth smiled at the others, who nodded in agreement.

"Oh, I'm ready, Seth. And then you and I can…"

Seth ignored her and began fumbling with the lock.

Sandra stopped speaking and then braced herself, with cleaver ready to strike.

"Okay, Sandra, here we go!" The doorknob made an audible 'click' noise as the key found purchase. Seth stood back from the door.

Sandra steeled herself, and then made as evil a face as she could muster.

"Oh, darling, it's time for our-"

Sandra grabbed the doorknob, twisted, and pulled the door open.

PJ was sitting on the toilet, but the lid was down. His pants were pulled up. PJ looked directly into Sandra's eyes. In his right hand and supported by his left was a .45 Magnum, the same kind Dirty Harry brandished while he asked a San Francisco treet tough if he was "lucky". The barrel was pointed squarely in the direction of Sandra's head.

"Midnight Kiss?" PJ asked. He pulled the trigger.

The bullet, a caliber that had been described by that same ginger-coiffed character as being capable of "taking your head clean off", entered Sandra's face just below the chin.

It exited the back and rear of her head.

Like a popped cork.

The crimson-colored champagne fizzed and flowed out from the newly made cavity in Sandra's skull. Her body tumbled backwards, until Sandra fell flat on her back on the kitchen floor.

"I really wish that Ex-Lax hadn't been necessary, sweetheart," he said, addressing Seth.

Seth walked over to PJ.

"I wish it were so too, sweetheart. But we had to make sure the bitch wouldn't see it coming, now, could we? Had to sell that sicky-wicky dear," Seth planted a deep, long, tongue infused kiss on his lover's lips.

Shannon elbowed Vernon. Now *that's* a midnight kiss, the gesture said.

Vernon began quietly singing *Auld Lang Syne* again in reprise, while Shannon looked on and smiled in joy for her friends, finally able to freely express their love for each other.

Shannon and Vernon then made their way over to Sandra's body with the champagne glasses and filled each up with the blood now pouring from her head. They filled six glasses and waited patiently.

A moment later, Mac and Wednesday appeared. With him, the smell of smoke arrived as well.

"The rest of the regular guests have been told the situation and have left the building, friends."

Seth appeared concerned for a moment.

"Did Majorie get her…"

Mac reassured his friend.

"Yes, she did. Asked if you'd join her for *Osso Bucco* next week."

Downstairs, the VIPs had all been locked in the game room, where Mac had dumped three gallons of gasoline just prior to their herding therein/. Once they'd been secured, Mac set it ablaze. Jonathan and the other eight undesirables that didn't make the final cut were down there burning alive.

Seth handed Wednesday his glass, and the six of them drank deeply. Once finished, it was time to go.

As they made their way outside, grabbing coats and jackets that were not stored in the coat room, PJ was curious about something and had to ask his man his burning question.

"Sweetheart?""

"Yes, darling?"

"Did she ever suspect anything? I mean, ever?"

Seth turned to him and smiled."Well. I *did* try to tell her she was the champagne."

THEATRE DU

GRAND GUIGNOL

20 bis rue CHAPTAL TÉL.TRI. 28·34 M° BLANCHE PIGALLE

FEU DE BENNE

DIRECTEUR: DS VERNON

CINQ ACTES de TERREUR INDENIABLE

Ne Pas FUMER dans le THEATRE - Ce Sera STRICTEMENT Applique!

Acte Un.

Justin Riesman's life was falling apart. Despite his best efforts, every recent event he experienced went completely wrong. But Justin had this recent spate of shit figured out. He'd surmised that since there was no shortage of people in his life likely wishing to do him harm, get in his way, and otherwise sabotage him, it was only a matter of time before a few acted upon their desire. Justin had become used to that muted hate and resentment from those in his orbit over the years.

But on some days, he thought, it seems as if even God Himself wanted to watch him suffer. This run of events started three weeks ago, when Justin had been fired from his job - unjustly in his mind. His exit from his company did not occur all at once but seemed to begin the afternoon his boss Ron informed him that he'd been making some high-profile mistakes.

Mistakes like missing slides in briefing meetings for the CISO or disclosing confidential findings to customers these were blemishes that could not simply be ignored. Ones that screamed distraction, disinterest, and poor attention to detail. Justin dismissed each as he heard them, convinced that none were his fault.
It was that bitch Miranda, thought Justin. *Sabotaging me like every other jealous asshole in this place.*

Miranda Ellis had been hired three years after Justin. She'd began in an entry-level position an almost insurmountable number of promotions away from reaching the same pay grade and job title as Justin.

Since then, Miranda held steady and worked tirelessly, and thus she was able to knock out a step up the ladder at every one of her annual reviews. She'd impressed everyone from Ron to the overnight cleaning crew in the process. Meanwhile, Justin skated by at each of his yearly evaluations with less than spectacular, barely adequate ratings. As a result, Miranda had reached the same level, pay grade, and authority as Justin. The two of them now shared responsibility for overseeing Technology Compliance at Hydrology, much to Justin's chagrin.

Bitch had an answer for everything it seemed. Moreover, it always was the *right* answer. And Miranda was right a lot… but regardless of her frequent displays of superior aptitude and problem-solving, Justin convinced himself that she'd been fucking her way to the top, if only because her as much quicker than his. The fact was, there *was* no ascent for Justin, full stop.

When Justin shared his feeling that she was purposely undermining him to Ron, things went from bad to worse.

"I uh… am glad you brought that up, Justin. There's another matter I need to discuss with you..." Ron trailed off. He looked up at the ceiling, his signature move when he needed a moment to collect himself. You could always tell ol' Ronald was ready for an aneurysm when his mustache began to twitch like whiskers of an exceptionally nervous rabbit. "Do you mind shutting the door behind you?"

This was bad. Justin had already been sitting in his office getting read the riot act for a full ten minutes - and only then did Ron require the meeting to go closed-door? Justin complied. He got up from the metal folding chair facing Ron's desk like a child being sent to his room. He tapped the side of the door with the tips of his fingers, just hard enough to get it to smack shut against the jamb. From behind his back, Ron shook his head side to side, noticing the half-assed, minimum-effort way Justin went about something as simple as closing a door. To punctuate this latest mediocre performance, Justin then plopped back down onto his chair as if he'd been on his feet for hours.

Ron stood up and walked over to his window. Ron clasped his hands behind his back and gazed out into the afternoon sky. As Ron prepared to dish out a career-ending death blow, Justin's thoughts drifted away from the seriousness of his current situation to, all of things, Ron's chair. It looked like fine oak and leather, but Justin knew it was veneer and plastic imitation leather.

Just like Ron, Justin thought.

Even his chair was bullshit. Man who sits in a chair like that is probably missing a testicle. I could so do his job better than him.

Ron adjusted his glasses and smoothed his tie, as if these fidgets and corrections would buy him time. His mustache continued to twitch. He cleared his throat, steadying his resolve. He turned to face Justin.

"Its been brought to my attention that Miranda has opened a case with HR - sexual harassment, Justin. Her complaint… the statement she made… they don't paint you in a great light. Carol took the complaint, not Rick, Justin. Maybe you might have had a fighting chance to appeal with him, but not Carol. That woman applied for her first HR job before she hit puberty. Carol already has statements from four people in your department that corroborate Miranda's claims."

"Ron, you know that silly-ass broad-" Ron cut Justin off.

"*Enough*, Justin." Listen, for once in your life.

Ron pressed on through his clearly made-up, rehearsed speech. Once again, Justin's focus drifted away from the crisis at hand to immerse himself in what he thought was genius-level insight into what was *really* going on.

Shes obviously figured out a new tactic - pin all her mistakes on me.

We worked on the Cartwright presentation together so this is how she takes all the credit for it.

Twist a few innocent complements up and bring them to straight to Carol, to feed that estrogen-fueled ego of hers.

Those cunts do their scheming and plotting, and boom, Ron's ready to shitcan me.

With a scandal like shes probably concocted, anything that goes wrong with the Cartwright deal is all on me.

I get out of this, I'm gonna get that bitch.

Justin did not get out of it.

He'd already been locked out of all work systems by the time security escorted him back to his desk. He had to pack his things into a cardboard box while his coworkers silently gathered, and then silently gawked at him while his escort eyed him up and down for any sign of trouble.

Somehow, the fact that nobody said a word and just stood and stared at him made this experience that much more humiliating. He felt like a zoo animal, caged, de-clawed, and rendered helpless - instead of being treated as he felt he should.

With some goddamned sympathy and respect, he thought. The moment he'd finished gathering his personal effects, that asshole guard took him by his elbow and escorted him directly outside, leaving him no opportunity to say anything to anyone. The security guard took Justin's key card badge, flashed a menacing look as if to say go ahead, give me a reason asshole, and then walked back inside. Justin watched as the door slowly swung shut and he heard the electric lock automatically engage, announcing the finality of the subject with sharp punctuation.

Acte Deux.

A couple of weeks after his dismissal from Hydrology, Justin's wife Beth suddenly and unceremoniously left him – second in the series of unfortunate events that transpired near the end of Justin's life.

He'd been fired on a Friday - Ron followed Carol's HR handbook to the letter on this; its less conspicuous, plus it gives the recently fired the weekend to calm down so as to *not* come in the following day with an automatic weapon and a bone to pick.

Not that it mattered for Justin.

She'd started packing also on a Friday. By Saturday night the kids' toys were packed, the clothes stowed in brand new suitcases. And all by the time he woke up on their couch, sleeping all day after drinking until seven in the morning.

He concluded, rather quickly, that it couldn't have been catalyzed by his sudden unemployment. Beth had the kids packed up far too quickly within a mere thirty-six hours. In that interim of time between the two, she'd never once mentioned his former job.

It wasn't the firing, so what was it? Was Beth having an affair?

She had moved into a place just across town, not needing a temporary place to stay - like with one of her imbecile friends or those wackjob parents of hers for a while. It takes time to pick out a new place, especially one suitable for children, so she must have been planning her exodus for some time. He deduced she'd been checking out potential landing pads while Justin was at work.

I've done everything for her and our children. Ive sacrificed so much.

He couldn't fathom why shed decided to leave.

He'd been a loving, devoted husband.

He'd been a terrific father. When Emily came just two years after the wedding, he'd been ready and had been there for them without fail. Another two years later their son, Tommy was born. They hadn't planned for him, but every family had a kid that slipped past the goalie, so to speak. His kids loved him, so he thought. He couldn't understand why she would do this to him.

Had to be having an affair. No other explanation made sense.

"Why would she break up the family like this? he thought, No. Who am I kidding? Not break up the family. More like cut me out of the picture, because..."

Watching his children's reactions as they walked out their front door to the car did not make him feel any better, only worse. They weren't fighting it, they weren't upset, they didn't beg their father to help or convince Beth to stay, or even to plead with her to stay with him instead, at least for the time being. They didn't *do* much of anything at all.

At last, he just asked them point blank what their reasoning was.

"You're just going to get up and leave the home you've lived in your whole lives? For what?"

Just the chance to get away from me, came the thought immediately after asking, since none of them had chosen to answer the question and remained silent instead.

The children didn't make eye contact when they each mumbled their own barely audible:

"Bye, Dad."

He couldn't keep his anger in another second.

"This is the thanks I get?" he yelled after them as the car backed out of the driveway.

"Guess you hate me like everybody else, like those assholes at Hydrology? Ha! You're all no better anyway. Just three more of you out there lined up against me. You're just another drop in the bucket."

The car began to pull away. Justin jogged out after it, screaming the last sentiment at them to ensure they understood their place now.

"ANOTHER DROP OF PISS IN A BUCKET!!!"

A week passed. He still had no idea as to why Beth had left.

Two weeks. Three.

Time went on, and as it did the reason grew less and less important. Justin's resentment pushed everything else into irrelevance.

None of this is my fault. They're all just ganging up on me. Easy target.

They all know Ill just take it, because in the end... I'm a good man.

A month passed.

Acte Trois.

For a man that always thought he'd have been better on his own, the next few months spent almost entirely alone did the proverbial number on him. His daily routine consisted of getting up in the morning, and then staring at the TV until at least noon; drinking coffee after coffee, served black with no sugar for every cup, ensuring his ulcers would only continue to widen and expand; and when the coffee began to fail in combating the exhaustion and the lethargy that only grew worse each day by comparison Justin graduated to methamphetamine abuse – this last nadir reached through a bogus ADHD diagnosis from a friend of his.

Justin's job search had also progressed along the same downward trend as physical and mental wellbeing. He'd implement a sound strategy like including applying to any jobs he found that even tangentially touched upon his unique and specialized competencies. But even with adopting that expansion of his search parameters, there were only a few viable opportunities that came along. And then, Justin's penchant for self-sabotage would kick into overdrive at precisely the worst time.

His pride would not let him consider a position that mandated or included a title change more junior than the one he'd held at Hydrology.

Anytime he'd see a requisition or posting online, or on job pages, for a spot lower than the one he'd held – the one *Miranda* also held, Justin would dismiss it without even a second thought.

The monotony of his routine and the repetition of applying for jobs he'd never land eroded his emotional regulation, eliminated his self-control. In one thought, Justin was the penultimate victim. In the one that followed, his general superiority as an individual, at least to everybody around him seemed so very apparent. And in the one after that, the blame for his current state of limbo was doled out by the armload.

"That bitch Miranda."

"Ron the coward."

"Backstabbing Beth."

After seven months, Justin's basic survival instinct had had enough of the wakings mind self-destruction. It told him: *you need to get away. Now.* And if there was anyone that Justin would listen to, it was himself.

Within moments of agreeing to his subconscious minds' urgent imprimatur, Justin decided upon a solo camping trip to Wampatuck State Park - just twenty or so miles from his house. He knew the woods quite well, after countless excursions therein while he'd been a Boy Scout. Would have made Eagle Scout too, were it not for his Troopmaster's kid being such a pussy having the old hand in warm water, piss your sleeping bag prank. But that was another story, another time.

Despite not actually having gone camping since those days as a scout, Justin was confident in his ability to spend a few nights camping and backpacking, away from everyone and anyone conspiring to bring him down. The solitude found in a natural environment would be a rejuvenating experience – enough to get his head screwed on straight at last.

He packed his things. A tent, a sleeping bag, food in a soft cooler with a shoulder strap, cooking supplies, spare clothes, a field guide, a rope, a Zippo lighter, some water, some whiskey (okay a lot of whiskey), and his favorite fishing pole – the one inscribed with *Fisher King* above the reel. The inscription on the pole was his fathers' favorite movie, and when he'd given the pole to Justin, he urged him to watch it some point in his lifetime. Justin's father had said:

"Its important to try to see things how they are, kid - not how we want them to be, or how we think they are. They're almost never the same thing." Justin had never bothered to watch the movie. Once he'd found out Robin Williams was in it, anyway. He hated Robin Williams.

After he loaded all his gear into the trunk of the ten-year old Toyota Corolla Beth left behind for him to use, Justin lit out for Wampatuck. The Corolla was old, but still reliable. Of course, this made him think about how Beth had taken off with their new, extended SUV because she needed it *for the kids*. He didn't mind back when they made the purchase; they had the money. Justin had been making the financial sacrifice for the family. But then, as Justin discovered the right blinker no longer functioned at a stoplight, thought about what Beth would be driving around at that moment. He slammed his fist against the steering wheel. "That's why it has all the new features and accessories and painted specialty-custom-order-metallic-*fucking*-blue, Beth!!! Oh, and lets not forget those heated leather seats. Really helps with getting the kids to their after-school activities. Right, Beth? Right?!" he screamed. The light turned green.

His car had been sitting in the sun in the driveway right up until he'd left and as soon as he'd got in Justin had been sweating. He cranked the air conditioning to combat the midsummer heat, though its effect was like a fan placed next to an open refrigerator. Beth had struck again. She was supposed to have taken the Corolla in to have the A/C recharged. Obviously, that never happened.

"But the marriage falling apart was my fault? Definitely my fault when you can't even handle little shit like an A/C, right Beth?!"

This outburst occurred roughly five minutes into his drive. By halfway, the screams included but were not limited to:

Beth, Ron and Miranda, his kids, his parents, Beth's parents, his coworkers, his friends, other drivers and pedestrians, and the woman in the green Mazda that idled next to him at another stoplight closer to Wampatuck. In the solitude of his car, the only response was the ragged breath of the A/C.

By the time he parked his car in the lot on the edge of the state forest, Justin had reached apoplexy. He squeezed the steering wheel until his knuckles turned a sheer white and screamed. Without words or meaning or thought, he screamed. He punched his fist into the interior roof, and he screamed. It felt good. He leaned his head on the steering wheel, almost burning from his grip and the sun through the windshield. He stayed like that, hunched over and breathing heavy. As his breath returned, he thought, "This. This right here. This is what I need. This feels good."

Feeling focused for the first time in months, Justin got out of his car, grabbed his gear, slung it on his back, and headed off into the woods. He walked a few miles in, sticking only to the main trails. He didn't see many passersby as he did, but he knew there must be more people out here somewhere because he'd seen quite a few other cars in the lot. Not running into anybody else on this hike suited him just fine though. It'd been quite a while since he could enjoy the solitude.

He listened intently to the sounds of nature around him - chirping birds and small animals dashing through layers of fallen leaves. He considered how there were no voices, no people. And with no people around, it meant that there was nobody to blame him for everything, to tear him down, or use him to further their own interests.

Eventually, he veered off the trail and up into the hills. He soon found a clear ledge that he could set camp on. It was wide, flat, and mostly devoid of vegetation, overlooking a huge swath of the forest and the park. Still, there were a few smaller trees on the perimeter of this ledge that he could use at night to raise his supplies off the ground – he could use a branch and rope to keep them out of reach from bears and other critters. Quite proud of himself, he felt every bit the Eagle Scout he should have been.

Justin noticed the summer sun creeping towards the horizon far to the west and knew he only had a few hours of light left. He cleared an area for his tent, wiping away rocks and debris so he wouldn't feel them in his back as he slept. He dumped the tent from its bag and began the tedious assembly. It took longer anticipated, but eventually it came together.

He got to work on building a fire. He chose a spot near the edge of the rocky shelf - it would look nice against the backdrop of trees reaching up from the forest below. He gathered twigs and branches and underbrush for kindling. He built it into a square base with the kindling in the middle. Then, for good measure, he built "one of them tepee tents," as one of his buddies in his troop called them, of much larger branches around and above that. He pulled out his Zippo, sparked it, and brought it to the kindling. The dry wood caught in a flash. It was up and going in no time and blazing higher than most would feel comfortable with for a campsite fire. Justin felt himself enough of an expert to handle it, however. He made himself a man's dinner – hot dogs and beans.

And then, it was time to truly be at one with nature. Do some real healing.

Justin pulled the bottle of whiskey out of his pack. He enjoyed the fire and the drink and the view. He smiled at the woods, and he cried with the stars.

He screamed into the night and was pensive with the fire. He slammed his fists on the ground and laughed at the moon. He gave into every base emotion as they surfaced. It wasn't long before Justin became simultaneously exhausted and inebriated, so dragged himself into his sleeping bag. Sleep came immediately and was utterly dreamless.

When he finally woke up, bleary-eyed and hungover, Justin felt thirsty – so incredibly thirsty. But no, more than just that. His throat hurt, ached as if he had been yelling or chain smoking all night. He knew he had done *some* yelling last night, wildly screaming names and obscenities into the sky but not enough to justify this sandpaper throat. He'd never smoked even so much as a single cigarette in his life. Confused, he figured that he would just get some water from his pack and worry about the why of this later.

But as soon as he opened the tent, the answer to that question became immediately apparent. He had been breathing in smoke all night, but not from any tobacco product or something similar.

Everything below the ridge he had camped out on had become a charred hellscape. While he slept off his whiskey drunk, the forest below had caught fire. The ridge he'd slept on remained safe. The only area that seemed to have taken any damage was…and then Justin realized what must have happened.

His campfire. He hadn't put it out last night. It had collapsed and fallen off the ridge into the arid, drought-blighted, summer forest below. Justin began to pace and mumble to himself.

"Why did the park rangers let people come out here when everything was so dry? Shouldn't they know something like this could happen?" He paced faster and faster, spoke louder and louder. "Shouldn't they at least warn people?! How could they let this happen?!" The thoughts became screams as fast as they appeared in his mind.

Finally, Justin slumped over on the ground next to the cooler he never actually got around to raising up into that tree. Hoarse from the smoke and from even more yelling, he grabbed a bottle of water and greedily gulped it down trying to clear his throat and his thoughts. He concluded that he'd be stuck here a while before he could attempt to make it through this desert of charcoal and ash.

He knew that he had packed for a few days so he shouldn't run out of supplies.

The remnants of the fire seemed to be moving away from his position. If that kept up, he'd be okay. Justin laughed. The only thing left here to burn was himself.

The thought never crossed his mind that while the fire moved away from him, it moved towards the town.

Justin remained in place for the day. He passed the time however he could. He watched planes drop Phos-Chek in front of the fire line to try and slow its progress. He watched helicopters drop countless gallons of water, stolen from lakes and swimming pools in the area. Occasionally, the wind would shift, and he would have to cover himself or hide in the tent to avoid the smoke. He found his old field manual and read it until the sun disappeared.

Justin decided against lighting a fire that night. He ate a cold dinner, drank some more whiskey, and occasionally watched the wall of destruction do its final work off in the distance.

Time dragged on through the night, just him and the dancing light of the distant flames. Despite the whiskey, sleep remained elusive. He laid down and got back up over and again, pacing with increasing annoyance. Finally, just before dawn, a fitful sleep took him.

There was a dream.

Justin stood at the front of a surreal, misty lecture hall. Every seat in hall was filled. Most of the faces were blank and without features in his dream state. He did see his family - Beth, Emily, and Tommy. He saw Ron and Miranda, as well. They stood up silently. They raised their arms in unison and pointed directly at Justin. The rest of the crowd then followed suit. Silent, staring, pointing, judging. All at once their jaws fell open and all at once, they began to wail. And for a moment, they looked as if they had all caught on-

He woke with a start. Even in sleep, he thought, he couldn't get away from those blaming him for things that were not his fault. His head throbbed and he was still very tired. The sun had barely begun its ascent into the sky, making it clear he had not slept long. But he knew he was awake for the day.

Climbing from the tent, he began to assess his surroundings. He looked off in the direction of the fire but noticed he could not see flames anymore, only smoke. Perhaps in the early morning hours, the firefighters had gained control of the situation.

He sighed, "About time."

Whether they managed to fully put the fire out or not, it seemed time to pack up his things and try to find his way out of this flame-ravaged forest.

Acte Quarte.

Justin climbed down the ridge and into what was left of the woodland below. It had burned down to ash and to the dirt in most places. What remained of trees stuck jagged from the forest floor like the broken ribs of a long dead fire giant. Anything left of actual wood glowed still as dying ember, pulsing, and flickering in time with the wind. Small patches of fire dotted the land, horrible braziers of sacrifice and ruin.

Justin knew the trip back to his car would be dangerous. He did what he could to pull back loose clothing and kept his remaining water close at hand, for all the good it would do. He tied an extra shirt around his nose and mouth.

Ash kicked up on the ground as he walked through it, swirling like grim confetti and making it difficult to see. He'd thought he was heading back toward the area where the path was, only to be forced to double back or veer wide to get around areas that were still ablaze.

Despite his surroundings, Justin's thoughts drifted back, once again, to his firing at Hydrology. All at once he realized what it must have been that got him on unemployment line: it was his compliments about her dress and her smile one day (compliments that at the time she had seemed more than delighted to receive) that she threw back in his face, to further her own goals. He wondered how many other innocent guys must have already been the subject of her machinations.

"And what better way than showing bravery by overcoming the sexual harassment of a peer? Even better if you can make that peer look incompetent too. Fucking bitch." Justin said this aloud while stepping over the charred remains of a squirrel caught by the flames.

He thought about how his wife looked at him with disappointment, but not with surprise, when he told her he'd lost his job. Beth had expected him to fail; he could see it in her eyes. She didn't even seem to hear the part about him being set up. Then he thought about how she left saying that this had been coming for a long time. There were signs she said he should have seen. Obvious ones, she'd said. But he had never seen them and was taken completely by surprise. She had said "You aren't here even when you're here," whatever that meant. He felt like she had spoken in riddles just to confuse him.

"How can I be here and not here, Beth? Listen to yourself!" Justin said this aloud as a once-proud oak collapsed to the ground, having sustained too much fire damage at last.

He thought of his kids. They seemed to blame him for everything, as well. He loved them, of course, so he didn't know how this had come to be the way of things. He didn't think he punished them more than their mom did, or somehow unfairly. Come to think of it, he hardly ever punished them at all. Beth did all that. He rarely ever saw them on most days, even before their mother took them across town. They had spent so much time in their rooms on their games or their phones or whatever it was they were doing. Strangely, the only time he felt their absence since they left was when he was eating dinner alone.

He had started down a hill that had ash piled deep and loose. The ash slid and his footing gave way. All at once he was falling, tumbling down the hill in the burning woods. Somewhere in the chaos of the descent, he heard *Fisher King* snap. By the time he came to a stop he was cut up, bruised, and singed. He laid sprawled on his back, staring at the sky as embers rained down like crematorium cast-offs.

He found that he had fallen into a natural alcove made so by a collection of boulders. The boulders followed the path of the hill he had just fallen down, and then cut across in front of him, making an "L" shape. As he stood up and began brushing himself off, he noticed something that looked out of place tucked in the corner of the rocks.

He approached slowly, a rising sense of dread working its fingers around his throat, making his breaths shallow and quick. The dread knew what Justin would see, even before he did. But when he did finally get a clear view of what hiding in the shadow of the boulders, he began to retch.

In the alcove, there were two charred bodies and what remained of them after the fire took them. So intense was the heat here, dead in the middle of the fire that all that was left of these people were blackened bones, and even the bones themselves had begun to be consumed. The larger of the two bodies cradled the smaller one, as if trying to shield it from the flames. They had given their life in an act of protection, that unfortunately, was just not enough. Justin realized that one set of the remains belonged to a child.

Justin backed up, gagging at the smell rising in the air, like burnt pork and liver, ammonia, and worse, something that tickled his nose with sweetness. He shoved the t-shirt into his face, doing anything he could to block the smell. A tree stopped his backwards progress. He leaned there for a minute, trying to get his bearings, and trying not to vomit.

All he could think about was how he needed to get out of these woods. How he needed to find his way back home. How he needed to get his life back to normal.

All at once, Justin realized that the tree he was leaning on still glowed like a charcoal pit for most of its surface. He jumped forward, his backpack having caught fire. He threw it off his shoulders as it smoldered and smoked. He managed to get a bottle of water out of his cooler and put the small backpack fire out. When he lifted the bag up to assess the damage, the front face of it gave way and all his supplies dumped onto the forest floor. In that moment, Justin felt part of himself give way, as well. The last useful parts of his mind seemed to fall out as well.

The cooler had also ripped in the fall. Justin jammed what he could into his pockets, water, the whiskey, some packages of jerky and a granola bar.

Slowing down now would be a bad decision, he thought. *Almost as bad as bringing a child camping this far in the woods.*

After hours of trudging through the wasteland, Justin finally started to recognize his surroundings. He had made it to what was once the far end of the trail where he'd strayed from it, at the beginning of the trip. He headed back towards the entrance, using the path as guidance when he needed to go around further obstacles.

Exhausted, he made it at last into the parking lot. His relief was short lived though. His car, along with the one other car still left in the lot, were burnt beyond usability. The tires had popped and melted into the asphalt. No glass remained in any of the windows.

He stared at his car wondering if the destruction of that old thing would net him any insurance payout. "Probably not even enough for a decent down payment on a new one," he said to himself.

Dejected, he looked at the other car. What appeared to be the remains of a coffee travel mug sat in the front seat cup holder. Mom or Dad had been tired. The back seat was scattered with melted plastic toys and burnt up stuffies. The top right portion of a teddy bear's head endured, waiting patiently on the floor for the return of someone who would never come. Its remaining eye stared up at Justin. He looked away and sighed.

He'd have to walk home. When Justin, reached the exit of the lot, he sighed again. Something had collapsed in the fire, making a simple egress impossible. He doused a sturdy looking portion of this obstacle with the last of his water, and then untied the extra t-shirt from around his face and threw it on the pile, shielding his hands from the remaining heat as he vaulted over. Landing on the other side, he took the shirt and started walking again.

A more observant person might have seen this pile of wood and metal for what it was: a large sign previously assembled by the park rangers, warning of an extreme risk of forest fires.

He wandered into the streets heading back in the direction of his house. This part of town, the part where Beth and the kids had moved to, had been destroyed. The wooden husks of buildings still stubbornly glowed and smoked. Orange and yellow flowers on the grave of a dead town. Justin had no idea if Beth and the kids had made it out. He found it strange that he didn't care one way or the other.

Hours later, when at last he turned onto his street, he was shocked to see that the fire line stopped dead just there; it had finally been contained just before it reached his house. All of the houses on his street looked exactly as they had when he had left two days before, apart from being darkened by soot.

He didn't know how to process this information in his exhausted state, so he didn't bother trying. He just stumbled up his front walk, let himself into the house and collapsed onto the couch. The sun was low in the sky and in no time, he was asleep, pushing away the horrors of the last few days. Blissfully, there were no dreams this time, only darkness.

Acte Final

When we see things for how we think them to be...

A loud thud woke Justin from his sleep. It was dark, even darker than normal. There was no electricity to be had anywhere for miles, so no streetlamps, no random appliances, and their overnight glows. While he could not see the clock, he knew it must be the middle of the night. No hints of dawn presented themselves through his windows.

Waking up on the couch, Justin was disoriented. More thuds. As he gathered himself, he thought that it sounded as if they were coming from his front door.

"Who the *fuck* is coming to my house in the middle of the night?" he asked aloud. More thuds answered his questioning, insistent that they were answered.

In his weariness, Justin failed to register the banging on the door did not have the cadence nor rhythm of an actual knock. There was no pattern to the sound, they were just sporadic, singular hits made his either a palm or fist. Justin also failed to notice the dim light shining at the edges of the front door.

As he reached for it, the door burst open, throwing Justin back into the room. He looked up at the open passageway to see three mangled corpses shambling their way in. They were severely burnt -their flesh shriveled, blackened, and split into countless fault lines of char and ash. Deep within the cracks of their skin he could see still-burning embers, glowing a deep orange like lava under a blackening crust. As they moved their skin made noise like a wood set aflame, flaking, and shifting in a settling campfire.

Justin was paralyzed with fright, his mouth frozen agape.

In seconds, they seized Justin by the arms, setting his biceps to burn the second they took hold, their fingers leaving scorches like a hot grill grate on a raw steak. He screamed as the smell of singed arm hair evolved into the nauseating sickly-sweet smell of burning flesh.

It wasn't until they brought him to the ground before he realized who they were. Who else could it have been? It was Beth, Emily, and Tommy. Mercy would have made them unrecognizable, but there was no mercy to be found here. His wife, his daughter, his son, all disfigured, monstrous forms of their former selves. The eyes in their skulls had burst from the heat. Their noses and lips and ears were no more. But there was no denying who they were.

Beth's distinctive gold and garnet necklace that she never took off had melted into her chest.

Emily's braces reflected in the glow. *Green and pink, green and pink, green and pink, rubber all melted to her teeth.* Like a nursery rhyme! Justin began to cackle, as he began to sing it aloud, louder and louder and…

"GREEN AND PINK, GREEN, AND PINK! RUBBER ALL MELTED TO HER TEETH!"

"GREEN AND PINK, GREEN, AND PINK! RUBBER ALL MELTED TO HER TEETH!"

The blood rolling down their faces boiled and steamed. Justin screamed as his children plunged their burning hands into his tender abdomen, clawing their way in, roasting his bowels, kicking up a putrid stench of vinegar mixed with shit. He spasmed and began coughing up blood. The world swam as his entrails spilled onto the floor. His children buried their faces in the viscera, chewing like hungry street dogs on a tourist's dropped meal. Beth leaned in close as if for a kiss. Instead, she clamped her teeth down on his esophagus, pulled back, and showed the room in red. His screams were replaced with the futile gurgling of a drowning man. The burning corpses of his family laid down on top of him, and Justin burst into flame.

When we see things for how they are….

Police stood near a dumpster behind the 7-11 on Stevens Street. The rookie was off on the side of the building throwing up. He couldn't handle the smell. Behind the barricade two detectives talked over what they had found.

"Set of clothes. Folded neatly outside the dumpster. Cellphone. Wallet. ID says 'Justin Riesman.' Mostly empty bottle of Jim Beam. Fully empty container of gasoline. Zippo lighter was melted into the palm of his hand.

"Suicide?"

"Couldn't be any more obvious. Although why in the fuck somebody would pick lighting themselves on fucking fire is beyond me."

"You didn't read the file? Fired for sexual assault from his job, wife left him and took the kids months ago."

Inside the dumpster, the burnt body of Justin Riesman sat, curled into a fetal position.

"What's that in his left hand?"

"Dunno," the other detective leaned in to get a better look.

In that hand a picture had survived Justin's self-immolation. A photo of happier times, Beth and the kids and him, taken on an ocean bluff. The picture had endured amazingly well, aside from the curled edges and the spot Justin's flaming thumb had covered. The spot on the photo with him. His family smiled on, while the picture of Justin…

...and the real Justin just burned away

TOURNÉE DU THÉÂTRE
DU
GRAND GUIGNOL
DE PARIS
C. CHOISY directeur

LE JARDIN DE GOMORRAH

DR. SN HUMPHREYS

TOURNÉE DU THÉÂTRE
DU
GRAND GUIGNOL
DE PARIS
C. CHOISY directeur

Acte Un.

Big Martha had lived at the house on Dooley Road for thirty-six years, yet only now could she finally tend to her very own garden. In the early years living there, the garden had been a playground - meant for children. It had shiny swing sets and painted wooden playhouses and a big plastic sand box that the sand rarely, if ever, stayed within its confines. And all of these *accoutrements* stood upon brilliant, thriving Kentucky bluegrass – the only actual aspect of her backyard that could considered garden-like. But then, as those thirty-six years rolled along, the garden-slash-lawn became more and more of a chore to maintain, especially as age took its inevitable toll upon her and Don. And when the years really began their subtractions, the garden became more yellow than green, an all-too-apparent symbol of their declining health.

So Don ripped out the dying grass and put down the fake stuff. "Easy to care for!" he'd said. Martha despised it. Then Don disappeared, like the grass. Not to move on to someone and someplace else like the children had done years before. No, when Don left her, it had been the big C that took him.

It was not quick, and it was not easy for him. Or her.

Martha didn't want to sit in that house alone while having to look at a fake, dead plastic lawn. She missed life and vitality, and days gone by. Within a few days of Don's passing, she'd gone to the garden center and hired them to rip up that awful plastic turf and replace it with lush green sod. She bought a load of plants to go along with the new lawn - specifically to attract butterflies, birds, and bees. As she walked away from the garden shop, she felt a crippling pain in her back. It was a grim reminder she'd soon be rejoining Don.

But until that day, she would make her garden an oasis teeming with life.

The house itself was too big for Big Martha to live in alone, anyway. Three bedrooms, two baths, a living room, and a den. It was a lot to maintain for one person, let alone an elderly one, and it was too quiet: too empty. She decided that she'd do her younger sister a favor – she'd give her wayward nephew an invite to move in, almost rent-free.

Brian was the kid's name, and he had always been a loner. Brian was nearing thirty with blond-ish hair, a distractingly large nose, and a weak chin. Big Martha didn't care to admit it anyone least of all herself, but Brian was awkward if he was anything and socially stunted to boot. When she extended the invite, Brian had no friends, no job, and no prospects. So Martha went a step further, and when first moved in she got him an interview at the hobby shop downtown. She figured if he worked and paid something, literally anything towards her bills it might boost his confidence enough to get him out into the world and to take care of himself. Maybe even try to grow a beard to cover up that glass jaw of his and not look like an overgrown child.

The day after Brian arrived and had gotten himself mostly settled in, Big Martha climbed into her tiny little Volkswagen to make for the garden center once again. After an hour of carefully selecting the next round of additions to her garden, Big Martha drove home with a load of bulbs and *three* bird feeders. As the miniature buildings rattled around in the hatchback, their incessant wooden clicking and clacking together made her more and more impatient to really get to work on her backyard project. Now that Brian was in-house, she assumed he'd help her unload the car and carry her treasures out back to her burgeoning little ecosystem.

Big Martha pulled into the drive and rang the house phone from her mobile. "Brian, can you come out and help me unload the car, dear? That's a good boy. Thank you."

Brian *loathed* being called "good boy", even when he was a child. And now he was twenty-eight, and she still called him that. *For fuck's sake.* Aunt Martha had always spoken to him like he was a child all his life. He supposed that in her eyes at least, he must have appeared to her as one - at least compared to her ancient ass. But his father had been threatening to kick him out for the previous month and Radwell – where Aunt Martha lived - was a thousand times better than the shitty little town where he and his parents lived, moving in with the old bag was still a no-brainer. He'd just have to deal with being called 'good boy', at least for the time being.

"You coming, boy?" Big Martha called up from the front door. Brian shut down his laptop and headed for the stairs.

"Right away, Auntie," he called out.

"Fucking old hag," he mumbled to himself.

Brian took the steps as slowly as he could. He hoped that by dragging his feet as if they'd been fashioned out of stone or steel, she'd give up and just do it herself. Big Martha was wise to the game however, and simply waited at her chosen station. When he finally did reach the front door without nary another peep from his aunt, he knew that not only had his plan failed, but that she knew he'd do exactly as he'd done and had fully anticipated it. He opened the door and saw her walking back over to her shitbox German car, a giant smile on her face. She motioned over her shoulder for Brian to come hence.

"Just take everything from the trunk here and leave it on the back porch. I'll sort through it later. After you're done, I could make you a nice cup of tea Brian for your trouble." "No thanks, Auntie, I'll pass." In all the time he'd been old enough to drink the crap, she'd never relented in trying to shove her weak tea down his gullet.

Brian had made the mistake of taking her up on the offer just once, years and years before, and when he did, he saw that her tea appeared and smelled more like toilet water - cloudy and dull gray with a vague aroma of piss. The event was so traumatizing, Brian found that he could recall an uncanny amount of detail about it:

He'd been eleven when his encounter with Martha's bathroom-in-a-cup occurred, sitting at the very same table that still adorned her kitchen. Brian was staying with her and Uncle Don while his parents were off on an anniversary getaway. It was sometime after lunch, and he'd been munching chocolate chip cookies, reading a comic book, and generally minding his own fucking business. Aunt Martha made the same innocent-sounding offer then as she had just moments ago. At the time, it had felt very adult to take her up on it, to sit with her to presumably talk about…adult stuff. After seeing how it looked in the cup and smelling its acrid vapors seeping up into his nostrils, he balked at even drinking the "tea". Aunt Martha sat across from him, eying him presumably for his anticipated compliments.

It fucking tasted like hot sour milk. It was atrocious; so unbearable was the taste that Brian spit it out all over the comic book he'd been reading. Aunt Martha had laughed it off, but he'd paid for that book with his pocket money.

Maybe it wasn't just the tea. Maybe it was also her laughter.

Brian went out to the car and grabbed a bag full of allium bulbs and one of the bird feeders and headed through the kitchen area, out the back door, and out into the garden. He took in a deep breath through his nostrils. The air held the promise of spring. A bit damp, yet still it brimmed with the promise of a new life to come.

Soon.

He could hear the rising trills of birdsong from trees nearby, and while he listened, he found he no longer wished to do jack shit for *Big Aunt Martha*. Instead of placing the materials onto the porch as she'd requested, Brian dropped everything in place and headed back to get the rest. None of it, he determined, was making it all the way to the porch. It didn't matter in the slightest that the four-foot-nine woman her neighbors jokingly called Big Martha was too old and too small to even attempt any heavy lifting. He didn't move in with her so he could b her fucking day laborer.

On his way back to the car, Brian idly wondered if Little Martha, Big Martha's daughter (O, the irony!) still went by that nickname. Doubtful. She was few years older than he, but Brian hadn't seen or heard from her since she left for London over a decade ago. It was probably awful having the same name as your mother. Wasn't that kind of shit reserved for men? And what twentysomething who wasn't an MC Whatever wanted to go by the moniker "little" anything, anyway? He remembered trying to kiss Little Martha in the playground when it was still there.

Little Martha had knocked him out cold on the spot.

Once the car was emptied and Brian had run back upstairs to sequester himself in his musty pit of a bedroom, Big Martha went outside and began sorting through her purchases. The boy hadn't brought a single thing to the porch. Maybe he didn't understand. Not surprising. Still, she would carry on. The garden would carry on, as well. The bulbs could go in her box planters, which edged the entire back wall of the yard. Don hadn't bothered to turf under them, so they wouldn't need moving anyway. Martha hefted her bags of soil into the wheelbarrow that previously served as a decorative piece over the years, placed the bulbs on top, then wheeled everything to the back of the garden.

Big Martha felt that paralyzing pain again in her back, only elevated to near excruciating on this occasion. Still, she would carry on. The garden would carry on.

She didn't bother with gardening gloves - Martha loved the feel of the rich, fertile soil between her fingers. It was like, well, part of a ritual it seemed. She filled up the planter and began placing the bulbs gently in the dirt, patting the cool, damp soil around them. She thought about how lovely her garden would eventually be. Full of fresh flowers, green grass, hummingbirds and bumblebees, and butterflies. She thought she would even put out extra seeds, so squirrels would pay visit. Big Martha had always had a soft spot for wildlife, wanted them all to gather in her backyard in a celebration of life. Perhaps even Brian would come out of his dank cave when the weather began to heat up in earnest. She wouldn't mind a bit of human company, even if it was the runt of the litter, so to speak.

With all her bulbs planted, Martha took the wheelbarrow off to the shed. She readied the garden by clearing the turf's surface so the gardeners could more easily remove it. No use leaving extra work for them.

Brian looked out his bedroom window and scowled. He'd calculated then that he was going to be mowing the lawn Aunt Martha insisted on installing. More work on top of just regular work.

Tomorrow was the job interview she'd set up for him, so Aunt Martha left him to his own devices for the rest of the evening. Aunt Martha hadn't rifled through his things – yet. He imagined she would, at some point. If she had already, there would have been no job interview the following day. Big Martha would have cancelled it in a second.

He opened his duffle bag and pulled out the skins he'd picked out himself. They were the skins he would wear for his new life. Brian opened his laptop up again.

Acte Deux.

A week passed.

Brian woke up at noon, to find a note left for him from Aunt Martha. Mr. Collins had called that morning to tell Brian he'd gotten the job at the model shop. Brian was dismayed at this. This dumb fucking job was totally going to cut into his online life. He would, however, finally have some cash. There were quite a few things he'd been wanting to buy, and Brian figured he'd have enough time to save up for them.

Brian decided that the entirety of his last unemployed day would be devoted to quality time with himself, and the others. He went back upstairs, shut the curtains, opened his laptop. Before he could enjoy himself, he had plans to make, and people with whom to make those plans. That came first.

Aunt Martha spent the day and better part of the night tending to her garden. That came first as well.

People have their priorities.

The next morning, the gardeners Big Martha had hired arrived at an obscenely early hour. Hearing the commotion they made outside, Brian awoke, groaned, and rolled over, looking at the clock. 7 am. It was time to get up and get ready for his new job. He stayed in bed for another fifteen minutes regardless.

Halfway through his stolen grace period beneath his sheets, he heard Aunt Martha's voice echoing up to his room from downstairs, offering the workmen a cup of her vile tea. He felt for a fleeting moment that he should warn them not to accept a cup, like he was obligated to do so out of some baseline common decency. He couldn't, of course. Aunt Martha would get offended. They'd have to learn the hard way, like he had. Brian heard one of the workers' distaste emerge as a half-groan, half-wail. The fifteen minutes were up. Brian grabbed his work clothes and headed for the shower.

As soon as she had seen the van pull up with the men who'd lay down her new lawn, Big Martha set to making tea. She pulled out her finest English breakfast for all these nice boys that came to take away the awful plastic turf. Bags in cups, not too much milk, a bit of boiled water, jiggle with a spoon and promptly remove. Half a teaspoon of sugar and another jiggle. And thus, boiling hot dishwater wrung out of a scouring sponge was ready to be served.

"Erm, thank you kindly, Big Martha. Just let us set up outside. We'll be back in a jiff." The two gardeners hurried off outside and made themselves as busy as possible. Martha shrugged and made herself an instant coffee. She personally couldn't stand tea, but her mother had raised her to always offer it to guests. The fact that no one seemed to like it had never phased her in the slightest. One of the men came in to humor her and took a healthy gulp from one of the cups. The poor man must have had a stomach bug, because the sound he made after drinking her tea reminded her of the one a dying animal makes just before its passing.

Martha left the man to his devices and wandered into the lounge with her coffee. It was time for her favorite home and garden show, 'Growing Together'. The format of GT, as she liked to call it featured talented landscapers and gardeners who went to neighborhoods just like hers and did "makeovers" of people's yards. By the end of the program, they'd have an entire street looking like the front cover of a magazine. Big Martha idly wondered if sixty-eight was too old to start a new career as an amateur landscaper-slash-gardener. It seemed like it was physically demanding work, but she considered herself fit, despite her back. She could deal with the occasional back pangs. She got up and walked over to the kitchen window. From there, she watched the workers hefting massive bags of soil over their shoulders, trimming trees, and contorting themselves into Twister-like positions. After just a minute or two of spectating their labors, she thought, *sod that*. She giggled at her own joke. Maybe retirement was a better fit for her.

Brian stomped down the stairs in his blue button up work shirt and tan slacks. He grabbed a light jacket from the hall closet and poked his head into the kitchen.

"Well, here goes nothing!"

"Good luck, Brian, I'm sure you'll do a fine job."

"Thanks Aunt Martha. See you tonight."

He's a good boy, really, thought Martha. *A bit odd, but a good boy.*

Fucking old bag, thought Brian as he walked out the door.

Hobby Bob's had been a fixture of downtown Radwell for fifteen years. The proprietor, "Hobby" Bob Collins had opened it when he'd turned fifty, as an appropriate and not-at-all obnoxious expression of the stereotypical male mid-life crisis. Instead of buying a fast car and attempting to bed a woman half his age, he quit his nine-to-five office job and opened a cutesy up-jumped toy shop. Hobby Bob stock-in-trade became airplane models, miniatures and figurines, and tabletop gaming sets. He'd played Dungeons and Dragons since the eighties, and now was as good as time as any to let his "freak flag" fly. Least that what the kids said these days. These were the sorts of things that were apt to go into and out of popularity, but he knew there'd always be loyal fanbases. . Translated to pounds and pence, it meant that even in lean times, he would do all right.

But after fifteen years had come and gone, Hobby Bob was tired of running the place on his own. He wanted someone to hand the place off to not for his own vanity, but more for those aforementioned pockets of people, those secret tribes of one recreation or another. He'd start the new kid Brian off simple, with the odd task here and there and just keeping the place clean. If he worked out, he'd start handing off the bulk of the work to his new would-be protegee.

Brian arrived at eight a.m. on the dot. Hobby Bob smiled and nodded gruffly as the boy walked in, acknowledging his punctuality.

"Good morning, Mr. Collins. Good to see you again, I would think?"

"Brian! Fine day out today. Now, you won't be sad you'll be missing it working in here with Hobby Bob?"

Brian shook his head from side to side.

"Man of few words. I like that. Alright, follow me then. We'll start with organizing the stock in the back. There's a more than a few boxes to unpack today."

Brian followed the old man to the back room of the shop and dutifully listened as he explained his stocking system. Hobby Bob relayed the sorting and storage of packages and boxes to him as if it were an arcane and secret calculus. After ten seconds of the doddering old fool speaking to him like he'd never put a box away in his life, he wanted to pierce both of eardrums with sharpened pencils. After twenty, he wanted to pierce both of Hobby Bob's. Once Willy Wonka's dimwitted older brother was satisfied that Brian understood, he returned to the front of the shop and let Brian get on with it.

Brian realized that he detested old people. All of them. Their superior tone, their musty smell, and most of all, their fucking insufferable attitudes. He survived the rest of his first day mostly by periodically thinking about taking over the shop once his new boss died – which might actually be soon by the state of the man. Brian walked along the shelves and studied all the merchandise. He slowly made his way down the aisle, only to stop dead in front of some plushies. There was a purple bear with a top hat, a stripey orange tiger, and a brown and white bald eagle. They were all so…beautiful…pure…magic. Brian slowly began to stroke his sudden and almost painful erection over his slacks with one hand, while the other ran through the soft pile of the plushies. He came in his pants within just a few seconds.

There was a purple bear with a top hat, a stripey orange tiger, and a brown and white bald eagle. They were all so… …beautiful…pure… magic. Brian slowly began to stroke his sudden and almost painful erection over his slacks with one hand, while the other ran through the soft pile of the plushies. He came in his pants within just a few seconds.

Big Martha was overjoyed. The workers had rolled the new grass, and expertly cut to fit the surprisingly large number of odd angles present in her yard's perimeters. It looked even better in reality than it ever had in her mind's eye.

Their foreman told her to wait at least two weeks before mowing it for the first time –the sod will have safely taken root by then. It may look overgrown and wild before then, but under no circumstances was she to cut it. Moreover, he'd also told her to refrain from walking on it as much she could manage. She'd have to be extra careful during that time. Without another thought she decided Brian would have to be banned from the backyard until the rooting had taken place. The boy simply had too many issues with following instructions. Or honoring requests. She had no doubt that if she didn't take such a firm stance as she was planning to take, he'd ruin the grass before it took root. It was just the sort of thoughtless thing kids like him did. Kids. Why did she think of Brian as a kid? Brian was twenty-eight.

Brian was still at work when the construction crew departed for the day, so Martha took the opportunity to sneak into his room, but just to open the windows. She took great care not to go through, look at, or even disturb any of his belongings, but the room stank of B.O. and some other, sickly sweet, fetid odor.

Heaven forbid she find out that other odor originated from the unseen collection of semen encrusted socks underneath his bed.

She threw all the windows therein as wide open as they would allow. There was only a slight breeze that had picked up by afternoon, and Big Martha had to make the most of it.

An hour later, she snuck back in to close them before he returned. Honestly, Martha couldn't have cared any less about the contents of Brian's room. His business was his business, and he was a grown man. And yet she'd treated him like a child because he'd never shown himself to be anything otherwise.

Maybe she'd have to look around if that godawful swank hadn't vacated the area. Just to see what was causing all the olfactory commotion.

But when she'd entered, the room was significantly airier, and the smell had mostly dissipated. Good.

But would her nephew be able to detect the difference? She hoped he wouldn't notice.

She didn't want him to feel his privacy was violated. Did he deserve it though?

Better start on dinner, she thought. Brian was due home from work in a half hour, and she thought maybe it'd be nice to have a meal waiting for him after a full day of work. Try and bridge the gap between them, as it were.

In minutes, Martha threw together a meatloaf and banged it into the oven. The meatloaf would take forty-five minutes to finish, and that would give Brian enough time to get in, maybe shower and unwind a bit before eating.

Martha, she told herself,

you really are a good auntie.

Big Martha and Brian sat down to dinner together, and barely a word was spoken between them.

Acte Final.

After two weeks had passed, the sod had indeed taken root while Brian had brought home his first paycheck. It had been a Friday, and while it should have been a cause for celebration between the two, there was none to be had - for in those interim days, between the night of the silent meatloaf and that afternoon, while Brian went to work and Aunt Martha to her garden, whatever relationship they shared together prior to his moving in had nearly disintegrated altogether.

Big Martha owed it all to Brian's increasing isolation, one that grew more pronounced as those days wore on.

And, by the time Saturday morning arrived, Brian only poked his head out of his room to fill his plate or to take a dump. Martha suspected he was into some new-fangled computer nonsense, probably one of those interweb games that grown men played in their parent's basements, something like that. But he did gave her half his paycheck towards bills and expenses and such, so in the end, what difference did it make?

He's a grown man Martha, she told herself, *let him live his life however he pleases.* That's what she thought she was doing. Live and let live.

For the remainder of that weekend, Big Martha spent all of her time out in the garden, planting, filling the feeders, and watching the birds. After all, this was what she worked so hard for, and it was time to reap what she had sown, quite literally.

She'd set up a tripod camera outside first thing, ostensibly to try her hand at photography, but it had really been more of an excuse to maybe give Brian some space, so he'd at least feel comfortable enough to come out of his room.

Brian peeked out the window at his aunt, scowling at her the moment her back was turned. He'd agreed to give her half his damn check just to keep her nosy ass out of his business. It seemed to be working, at least so far. Brian turned from the window and laid back down on his bed. He connected to Aunt Martha's wireless network and entered the private chatroom.

Things were finally coming together. He found it hard to keep his disdain for Aunt Martha up, when he considered where things were heading, and how it was so very soon they would truly begin to head there. Life would really be everything he dreamed. He wouldn't have to hide himself – his true self – for much longer. A few more paychecks stashed away, then a meet up with his online friends. Everything was going to work out. The thought of having them all close to him, physically and not over a WiFi connection, made him just as hard as he'd been that first day at Hobby Bob's. And just like he did in that backroom, Brian began to stroke himself over his clothes as he thought about his future.

Martha settled into a bit of a routine thereafter, with her camera set-up and garden to photograph taking up most of it. Mornings were for hummingbirds. There were the three feeders in the garden, and Martha could sit at the kitchen table, outside on the patio to view all three, or get behind the lens to take some crisp action shots of whichever one her avian friends had chosen for the days' hangout. Since summer had nearly arrived, the patio won out more than her other two options. While Big Martha sat, wrapped in her dressing gown, she'd enjoy a single cup of coffee. She'd change the nectar out of one of the feeders per day and did so on a rotating basis, so she could predict which one the birds would flock to.

Such a beautiful morning, Martha thought at least once every morning, as she'd then stretch out and sigh. She'd then watch the little birds flit around, their wings an almost invisible blur.

Just lovely little birds.

Cr. Lenka Simeckova

DOUBLE FEATURE
PRESENTS
AN EVENING AT
THE GRAND GUIGNOL

After coffee, Martha would get dressed - only to head right back out into the garden. She'd have a project planned for the following day, most nights by bedtime Today's project was the installation of a bat corner. She headed to the far end of the garden and began planting Evening Primrose, Honeysuckle, and Soapwort, plants whose scents attracted those nighttime visitors. Mornings may have been for hummingbirds, but the nights belonged to the bats. If things went according to plan, she'd have her very own twenty-four-hour nature show.

Once everything was planted and fed and watered, Martha headed up for a shower. It was one of Brian's rare days off, so on her way there she knocked on his door to check he was alive.

"You okay in there, Brian hon?"

"Yup, Auntie, everything's fine." Brian called back, rolling his eyes as he did. She'd interrupted a special moment - he was just about to make his first significant purchase since starting at Hobby Bob's. It was his first, tangible, real action he'd be taking as part of his new life. He hit the "confirm purchase" button, and as he did, his stomach tightened into a knot and his brow broke out in a fine sheen of sweat. Brian had never accumulated, let alone spent, this much money at once. It was well worth it. His forehead dripped onto the keyboard. Brian laughed at his own anxiety.

He felt powerful. He was becoming.

They were coming.

Dinner time came, and much to Big Martha's surprise and wonder, Brian sat at the kitchen table with her. She didn't want to jinx anything by asking why he was sitting with her. She decided to make idle chit chat instead.

"How's work going?"

"Oh, it's fine. Simple enough, really. I don't mind it at all." Brian bit into a chicken leg, a bit too savagely for her tastes.

"I do have a favor to ask you, Aunt Martha." Bits of chicken flew out of his mouth as he spoke.

"Ask away, Brian. You know I'm just happy we're talking."

What could he possibly want, completely out of the blue like this?

"I've been talking to some friends about having a get-together, and I was wondering if I could possibly have them come around here?" Brian trailed off at the end, expecting to be rebuked.

Friends? Since when did Brian have friends?!

Martha's initial surprise played plainly across her face, but it was quickly replaced with a smile. She could feel herself beaming. This was exactly what she'd been hoping for. Brian had made friends, somehow, someway, and now he wanted to have a party. Could it be that Brian had truly taken that big of as step, as a person, and as a…man?

Martha almost leapt out of her seat to exclaim a full-throated yes, but at least managed to show a little restraint.

"Sure, sure, of course you can Brian. This is your home now too! How many people would you be having around? Do I need to make myself scarce?"

"Oh no, nothing like that Auntie! Maybe 5 friends. We would just hang out upstairs, you could do your usual looking out for bats and you won't even know we're there. It wouldn't be like a *party* party or anything. Just a little ritual we're trying to get going is all. "

"Well," Big Martha beamed, "it would be fine even if it was a party. But your get-together sounds perfectly reasonable, and your friends are welcome anytime. When?"

"Tomorrow night, if that's okay?"

The shocks just kept on coming. Tomorrow night? It was as short notice as it could have come, but again, the significance of this event couldn't be understated. Or undermined.

"Well…sure. Sure!" Big Martha exclaimed.

Brian smiled at his aunt.

They then finished the rest of their dinner in silence, Martha positively delighted her nephew was finally blooming socially.

Brian simply went over the plan in his head now that it was assured.

When they arrived at around six the following evening, altogether and not separately, they had been quiet and polite enough - but strangely, they had all gone upstairs to Brian's room. Six of them, including Brian, cramped in such a small area – such small, *smelly* area? Martha considered this yet was unphased. It was hardly surprising that when Brian did finally make some friends, they too were a bit on the secretive, shy side. Once they'd all gone up, Martha started preparing for her evening outside as was her routine. She made some sandwiches and a big jug of sweet tea and took everything out to the table on the patio. She nibbled her snacks and patiently waited for dusk.

Brian and his friends chatted away and laughed nervously. None of them were particularly social under normal circumstances, but they were together now, and they were a family. Finally meeting in person was both nerve wracking and exhilarating to each. They passed around books and took turns showing each other obscure websites. Obscure, as in the dark web. And by the time the sun finally vanished that evening, they were fully comfortable with each other. The time had come, and they were ready.

Big Martha held in a deep breath as the sky was cloaked in the midnight blue of the night. She'd been waiting for the bats still – none had come. She'd even added more floral incentives - Night Scented Stock and Cherry Pie. Finally, on this evening, this perfectly serene evening, she heard the flutter of wings. She looked up, and from their darkened, spirited shadow bolting across the sky like darkened fireworks, Martha thought she spied five, maybe six bats overhead! They circled, catching the scent of the flowers, then came lower, and then finally landing. Martha's breath caught in her throat. They were tiny! They flitted back and forth erratically, so different from the hummingbirds and larks and sparrows. Big Martha was overcome with awe.

And then suddenly, searing pain.

"Fuck you, Martha," a muffled voice spat out. She looked down at her midsection to see the tip of a knife sticking out, and a bloom of red spreading around it. It was a long, thin, yet cruel blade that had entered her back just to the left of her mid-spine. Big Martha fell forward, landing squarely on her face, tasting the sod as it struck the ground. She felt the knife jiggle around inside her sadistically, like a joystick for an arcade game. A mouthful of that wonderful sod muffled her scream. Someone pulled out the knife and rolled her over. The implement removed; Martha bled heavily into the grass.

As Big Martha felt darkness overtake her, she looked up to see a man, naked save for a giant, fuzzy, baby blue bear head. He stood over her, head cocked to the side like the RCA dog, holding the blood-drenched knife in one hand, and his cock in the other.

Brian?

Her last thought as the sound of the voice suddenly rang familiar in her mind. Brian licked the blood from the knife, and smiled as he kicked her head, jacking off furiously.

Big Martha opened her eyes. Looking down, she saw that her wound had been field dressed to stop her hemorrhaging.

They kept her *alive*? For…what?

She noted that she had been gagged, and she had been tied up. She scanned her surroundings. Her lawn. It had been chewed up, chopped up, ripped up, and torn asunder. Nothing remained except for a tangle of mud and grass. Martha was surrounded by what she could only liken as characters from a rejected children's show, perhaps even a group of failed team mascots. Of the four that she could make out, there had been a purple cat, a yellow dog, a red fox, and of course, her nephew Brian - the blue bear. All of them naked except for the giant furry heads they wore as if they were marching in some obscene parade, and each of them had smeared generous portions of her own blood all over their bodies.

From her left, she heard grunting noises. They were the sounds of…Martha twisted her head in the direction of the noises. There, on her patio two people, one adorned with the head of a horse and the other a rabbit mask, were fucking furiously, with zero abandon. She could tell that they were both men, and noted, her sanity dying faster than her body, that the horse had been tearing the rabbit's asshole up like her lawn had been while she was unconscious.

She turned away from the sight, to see that there in the center of her lawn, a giant circle had been carved, presumably with a stick. Or perhaps the knife that had been plunged inside of her. The fox, cat, dog, and Brian – no, the bear circled around her and began chanting:

"EVERLASTING LIFE, POWER EVERLASTING!"

Suddenly the no longer Brian blue bear lunged at her with his own blade, hacking wildly into her chest. It had been that first big purchase he'd made, delivered express overnight. Blue bear finally ceased his wanton stabbing, only to thrust his fingers into one of the holes, or perhaps all of them at once, pulling and wiggling them around until they found purchase. Blue bear yanked back towards himself, snapping her rib cage with a sickening crack. Big Martha screamed into her gag with her last, dying breath as the copulating pair on the patio's cries of ecstasy rang out in unison.

"EVERLASTING LIFE, POWER EVERLASTING!"

At last, Brian Blue Bear put his mask back on, and began rubbing blood onto Red Fox's breasts. Soon the six of them paired up and fucked desperately in Big Martha's quickly cooling pool of blood and viscera. They cried out in animalistic growls and howls, embracing the beasts their felt and fabric headgear embodied, and what they could only pretend they could be. Once all had been spent, they gathered in the corner of what used to be Big Martha's Garden and hosed off their costumes. They piled into their cars, and left Radwell in the dark of the early morning hours.

What the police found, when the police did finally arrive, had never been seen before in Radwell. Not ever. They found the vague shape made by Martha's dead body, splayed out on a circle with a triangle in the middle.

There were four points marked with lumps of Martha's coagulated blood, in each of the cardinal directions. Her half-eaten heart was left just next to her body, placed there purposefully, intently. One copper noted, just before feinting with sheer horror, that there were several sets of human bite marks. Her innards were spread out across the yard, half-eaten.

The police were obviously *very* eager to speak to Brian, but both he and his laptop had disappeared. Brian had also disappeared, even from himself.

Now, there was only Blue Bear.

The following day, Detective Inspector Sam Tyler - the lead assigned to the massacre - arrived at Hobby Bob's looking for answers. He found more of what they had found the previous night. Hobby Bob was in the stock room, surrounded by shelves torn from the walls, games and models smashed everywhere. His body was found all the way at the back, his head in a puddle of dried blood, a tiny figurine of a purple bear in a top hat rammed unceremoniously down his bloated throat. Tyler saw that the killers had cracked the back of his skull on the floor and forcefully inserted the bear, but still had taken the time to draw arcane symbols around his corpse in the blood.

"Whatever the hell all that is," Tyler mumbled, moving over to a pile of animal plushies nearby. They looked as of they'd somehow been left there on purpose. On top there was a blue bear. A Health and Safety Inspector arrived just as Tyler picked the bear up.

"UUUGHHH WHAT THE FUCK!" Tyler dropped the bear onto the floor almost as soon as he'd touched it.

"Something the matter, Tyler?" asked the HS man.

Tyler wiped the sticky substance on his fingers on his pants. He knew exactly what was the matter and could barely contain his disgust.

"Nothing. Nothing's the matter," Tyler answered. He turned to the HS Inspector.

"Got any hand sanitizer?"

LE THEATRE GRAND GUIGNOL

Les Falcons de la Nuit

dir. John A. McColley

Acte Un.

The black and white clock on the yellow wall of the diner ticks away seconds like they're flat notes from a broken instrument, letters that don't add up to words dropping out of a typewriter.

Tick.

The percolators bubble, water in drowning men's throats. The air is hot despite the hour, trapped in the city like the four people going about their business, trying to ignore one another as much as possible, but keenly aware of every movement, every breath.

Tock.

Jimmy rinses out mugs he's cleaned three times, just for something to do. No greater sin for the worker bee than to look idle. The others sit at the triangle of polished wood that forms the countertop that hemsming Jimmy in. A man in a light gray suit, alone, stares into his coffee as though it will solve his problems. A man in a dark gray suit sits beside a redhead in a red dress, the finest woman Jimmy's seen in his joint in months, but Dark Suit pays her no mind. They haven't spoken a word to one another since they came in and set down their suitcases.

"Just get in, or missed your train out?" Jimmy had joked when they collapsed into the seats they'd now occupied for hours, waiting out the night, it seems.

"Coffee, two," the man had responded, typical, no time for the little guy, but he had time now, didn't he? All the time in the world for a please and thank you. Still, the words, or even a smile of thanks had never neared his lips.

"Can I get anyone some pie? No ice cream, I'm afraid, cooler's on the fritz," Jimmy tries.

Tick.

"You said," Dark Suit says, ending all conversation again for endless ticks and tocks as the minute hand races the hour, catching it again before anyone dares break the silence.

A police car slides by, its spinning blue lights slashing the night, reflecting off the chrome fixtures, the coffee percolators, the napkin holders. Light Suit turns away from the light, pulling down the brim of his hat. Sensitive eyes? Or…? As much as Dark Suit gets on Jimmy's nerves, along with the heat and those damned mugs, Light Suit is even more of a mystery.

Tock.

Shrugging to himself, Jimmy takes the cash register key and retreats to the back room. Water surges and splashes into a well-worn mop bucket, building a layer of white foam as it churns. The water is hotter than the August night, and spray mingles with sweat, sliding down his arms into thick yellow gloves as steam curls toward the high storeroom ceiling.

Finally cutting off the flow, Jimmy jabs the rope mop into the unseen bottom corner of the bucket, shoving it through the swinging door back into the kitchen, then through to the lobby. The scent of disinfectant, stinging his eyes with its closeness, scratching like an animal, mixes with the smells of coffee, hot bodies, and cheap perfume. The slam of the door makes Dark Suit and Red Dress jump, but Light Suit remainsis absorbed by the depths of his cup. Jimmy suppresses a smile at this. **Tick.**

"Theh you ah!" a new, familiar voice grates on his nerves. "A/C broke again?" The woman, a few years older than Jimmy, hair done up in large platinum curls, stands in a long coat hanging open at the front, and not much more. She's selling, and has all her wares out to bring customers in. The coat is for closing up shop when the police roll around, or in case of rain. Not much chance of the latter.

"What can I say? Old man's too cheap to get it fixed proper. Just keeps calling Ham in to kick it when he feels like working," Jimmy says, greeting Greta with something approaching a smile. He doesn't want to encourage her too much. There are already too many people hanging around for him. This is supposed to be a quiet shift, lonely. Lonely he can deal with. Chit chat and all the extra work people present… "Coffee?"

"Scoop of strawberry?" Greta bats her blue eyes, slips a shoulder out of her coat.

"Cooler's out, too. It's all soup." Jimmy isn't having it. He's done with her after the last time. Of course, he's been 'done' nearly a dozen times now. Still, there isn't any damned ice cream.

"Could really use it. Hotter'n th'Devil's underpants out there. At eleven!" Jimmy shrugs.

Tock.

Pie. Coffee's all I got." Jimmy drives the bucket to the far corner of the diner, around Greta and Light Suit, Dark Suit, and Red Dress. White foam sloshes up over the side of the yellow bucket like a creature trying to escape its fate.

Water and disinfectant splash across the tile, pushing grit and a candy wrapper toward the green baseboard. Tide is coming in.

Tick.

"Aw, come on, Jim, don't be like that. I'm sure you've got more for me other than bean juice and day old pecans." Greta says, coming up behind him. Her breath is hot on his neck. He can feel her body heat on the back of his arms as she grows closer, even through his shirt.

"Take a seat if you want. I've got work." He tries to fend her off.

"Never stopped you before." He could hear the sly smile on her lips.

"I told you before, we're done," he tried to say quietly, but forcefully.

"'Done' shmun," Greta laughs. Jimmy can feel the color rising in his cheeks. It's bad enough, having her breathing right down his neck, teasing him when she knows the old man doesn't pay him enough to keep on with her. That she keeps coming around, flashing the goods at him, trying to get him to buy stirs him up inside. That there are customers watching… people who might tell the old man and get him fired… His grip on the mop tightens. Tick. His knuckles pop.

"That's right," Greta whispers so close her lips brushed his ear. "Get a good hold on that stick." Jimmy pushes the mop, creating another wave. He imagines Greta and the others cluttering up his diner being washed away. Clean slate. Clean floor. Time to breathe.

Something shatters, making Jimmy jump. He raises the mop defensively, flinging water across the couple nearest him. Greta sidesteps, remaining behind him as he turns. A scream and a grunt issue from Red Dress and Dark Suit, respectively. "Sorry, the- aw shit…" Jimmy says, seeing the coffee cup in a thousand shards scattered across the white and black checkerboard of tiles, brown coffee reaching out in every direction like a dead octopus beneath Light Suit's feet. The man himself shakes his head.

"Sorry, kid, long day. Long week. Haven't slept in…" His excuse drifts off as his eyes focus on something outside, or perhaps in his own mind. Jimmy glances but doesn't see anything in the direction the man stares. Plunging the mop back in the bucket, he picks his way around the mess.

Tock.

"You just stay there," he says. "Don't nobody step in it." In a minute, he's back from the storeroom again, armed with a broom and dustpan for the cream-colored ceramic, the diner's logo of a pie and steaming mug broken into three neat pieces, but the rest a razor-sharp jigsaw puzzle. A trail of small triangles of brown liquid leads from ground zero back to a booth by the door. High heels. Jimmy doesn't even have to look to tell Greta's lounging there, giving him a mischievous smile. Like he has time for her antics right now. He just shook his head, hand tightening on the mop, pretending it's her thin, porcelain, neck. *That's right, get a good hold…* Greta teases him from inside his head.

The pottery shards screech like fingernails on a blackboard as he draws them across the tile into the dustpan. Dark Suit visibly shivers. Jimmy feels the skin on his arms and neck crawl. Bits of off-white shoot across the dustpan, bouncing off the back and falling like teeth in a back-alley brawl. Once he has all the shards he can see, he puts the broom and dustpan behind the counter and goes back to mopping, seething at Greta, at Light Suit who now slumps over the counter again, staring at an empty saucer. Or maybe he's asleep. His back to Greta's booth, Jimmy hears a little giggle and the shriek of ceramic on tile before she swats his backside and runs to the door, step, screee, step, scree, door open, bell tinkle, slam.

Jimmy lets out a deep sigh. At least she's gone. He considers locking the door behind her, but the other three paying customers still sit at the counter.

Jimmy shoves at the tiles as though he could dislodge them, sweep everything away, this diner, this city, every heavy-breathing, sneering, suit-wearing last spec of confining, choking, modern life. He banishes the heat of the night, the exhaust that rolls in every time the door opens, the sirens he can hear again in the distance…

He tries to imagine he's on a farm, digging a hole, a row in a garden-plot, where he can plant seeds, see his work grow toward a future of some security. A hand on his shoulder brings him around, spinning to see Light Suit, deep, dark, bags under his eyes like he's been beaten, a weak smile and a finger pointing toward his empty saucer.

"Black."

"Yessir," Jimmy hears himself reply automatically, even more convinced he needs to get out of here. Zombie-like, he watches himself drag the mop to the bucket and set it in the brown, clouded, water.

He trudges around the counter as though the air has become a thousand times as dense. Every step takes all his concentration, all his will. At the corner, he wonders where he's going, what his goal is. He stops and looks around at the others, who all stare off into space. He could be invisible, or a ghost. What would a ghost do?

Tick. Tock.

A ghost would get revenge. Smash coffee pots, mugs, throw the cash register through the window, flip tables and knock over stools. He's a whirlwind, grabbing, grunting, shoving, heaving, sweating. So much sweat. It runs into his eyes, stinging, making him blink. He's still standing at the corner of the counter, just at the part that flips up to let workers into the long, wooden, triangle. He reaches for the counter, lifting it and letting himself in.

Jimmy pulls a new mug from the wooden cave beneath the percolators, one of a porcelain army alongside stacks of saucers like futuristic skyrises. Out of habit, he takes one of these, too. He lets the brown, steaming fluid dribble into the cup, nearly black on nearly white, roiling and splashing. Coffee spatters his hand, making him jump just a little, natural reflexes subdued by habit and experience behind the counter. To jump away meant to splash more, spill more, maybe on white pants, biting pale skin almost the color of the cup.

Jimmy carries the coffee two steps before seeing the saucer and remembering. He tries to sweep the one away and place the one in his hand, but Light Suit stops him, signaling that he should place the other saucer atop the first. Who was he? Why did he look so tired? As tired as Jimmy felt. The question flees as quickly as it forms. He doesn't care about them any more than they care about him. Letting himself out of his corral again, Jimmy drives the mop bucket back into the storeroom and dumps it into the work sink. He leaves the mop in the sink, unable to bring himself to rinse it out, and heads back toward the front.

As soon as he passes the door into the kitchen, he's aware that he's not alone. He rouses himself to look and sees Red Dress standing at the day-cooler, a stainless-steel monstrosity on squat spindle legs. White fog rolls around them now, over high-heeled shoes and the feet no longer confined by them.

"You can't-," Jimmy stumbles over the words as the redhead wafts cold air over her chest. He shakes his head

"You can't be back here," he manages, raising his voice.

"Oh! You startled me. I was just looking for any food… We missed lunch, and dinner was supposed to be on the train… I could cook it myself, and we'd pay, of course." The woman leaves off fanning herself and begins pawing through the paper-wrapped packages inside the cooler.

"Oh, you'll pay!" Jimmy says, the cold of the cooler not touching him, not pulling away the heat rising in his face. Sweat pours down his back as he picks up a meat axe from the thick wood cutting table. He hefts it, tightening his fingers around the wood handle and the metal sandwiched between, bringing it down on the woman's outstretched arm.

Chck! Metal strikes bone. Fffft! Blood fires out of an artery into the cooler, drenching dozens of white paper parcels, dripping, freezing on the walls, mingling with frost as the woman, eyes wide, pulls back and stares at him, unable to utter a noise. Jimmy strikes again, at the neck, chopping down through another artery and the windpipe at an angle. This time, the blood comes for him, turning his white uniform red in seconds as the woman stumbles back, falling in the narrow lane between workbench and cooler, clutching her wounded arm to her chest.

The meat axe slips from his fingers as he steps closer, looking down as the woman whose eyes are already glazing over. Her chest still heaves, seeming to lunge at him, call to him. Her good hand moves vaguely toward her throat as if to stop the bleeding, but partway to its destination, the hand drops back to her chest, then slides to the side as her elbow drops. Jimmy reaches for her, pressing her breasts into her unmoving ribcage. He feels his body react as blood pools around her, weakly spurting from her arm and neck onto the brown tiles, seeking the grout between squares to reach out farther. Breaking free of the spell, Jimmy pulls back, stands upright.

"Great, more mopping. Thanks a lot, lady."

Acte Final.

He steps over her and reaches down to grab her hands to drag her to the deep freeze, staring for a moment at her stilled chest, white hills smeared with crimson. His hands stray toward them again, fingers brushing soft, warm flesh. The bell at the front door tinkled again.

Eyes wide, he grabs Red Dress' hands and shuffles backward, opening the door to the freezer and hauling her through. He pushes her legs in and slams the metal door, then knocks a coat rack of white aprons which had avoided the fountains of blood over as he steps back. Jimmy reaches for it, red smearing across the pristine edge of one, then they're down, a newly fallen blanket of snow soaking in the near end of the crimson pool.

"Hey, customer out here," Dark Suit says from the door to the lobby. "Say, what happened there?"

"Ah, damn cooler broke down in the heat. Meat's melting all over the place."

"Helluva mess, but it's gotta wait. Maybe change your shirt, though. Look like you killed someone." Dark Suit vanishes from the wedge of light and it narrows as the door falls to, popping open on this side, then settling back.

Energized by adrenaline, or perhaps taking something back he had lost, Jimmy retreats to the storeroom and washes his hands, scrubbing away every trace of red from the cracks in his chapped skin, the creases between his fingers. Glancing in the mirror, he also rinses his face, then dons a new uniform from stacks of laundered shirts and slacks. He'd gotten his, and gotten away with it, so far. People could be so stupid. He just has to keep control and figure out what to do with the body in the freezer before morning.

At the door to the lobby, he stops for a beat, takes a deep breath and plasters a smile on his face before pushing through. Simultaneously, the small service bell by the register begins having a seizure.

"Good even-," Jimmy says, but the other, in a linen suit cut him off with a rapid fire order.

"Two coffees, one with two creams, two sugars, one with four creams, one FreeSweet, to start. Where are your menus? Menus? Do you speak English? Why are you just standing there, boy?" Linen Suit demands while a younger woman in a navy blue dress hovers behind him, looking bored. Jimmy takes another breath, then lets himself into the serving counter to start on the coffees. "Menus?" The man insists again.

"No food. Cooks are gone for the day. Won't be back 'til five for the breakfast rush," Jimmy says, drawing coffee into two mugs. "No FreeSweet. Sugar?"

"That's fine," the woman responds.

"No, any other artificial sweeteners? Have to keep her away from empty calories," Linen Suit says. Jimmy shakes his head.

"Not 'til Tuesday, if we're lucky. Deliveries have been-"

"I don't care about your problems. You don't have it, you don't have it. No sweetener, then," the man snaps and waves the young woman toward the wall of booths. She sits just where Greta had been. Jimmy smirks to himself as he finishes off the coffees, both with two sugars, with his back to the newcomers.

"Say, you seen my girl?" Dark Suit asks. "Went back to snoop for food a little while ago."

"Never saw her. Maybe she went to the restroom," Jimmy lies.

"Mm, they do that a lot, dames." Dark Suit lights another cigarette and drops his match into the ashtray with half a dozen extinguished butts and the matches that lit them. Jimmy sets the coffees down on the counter for Linen Suit, but he's already walking away. While he sits across from Navy Dress, Jimmy goes out of the corral again, picks up the coffees from the counter and ferries them to the table.

"Thank you," the young woman says with a small smile.

Linen Suit says, "Is that the right time?"

"It's the only clock in here, so I have to guess yes?"

"Are you being smart with me, son?" Linen Suit looks as though he's going to get up again. Jimmy feels the yolk of meniality settling on his shoulders again after a moment of freedom, of power. It seems all the heavier for the time without its burden.

"No, sir!" Jimmy says with his best *kill-them-with-kindness* smile. Not yet, not quite yet. Not in front of so many witnesses. Where were all these people coming from, anyway? And why can't they just drink their coffee and leave? Jimmy returns to the serving space and begins writing up tickets for the coffees. He doesn't fill out totals yet. No one seems ready to go, as much as he yearns to check them out. He clips each lined paper to a metal bar along the edge of the counter by the register. Three tickets open at one am… On a Thursday!

He checks the percolators and finds the one not bubbling coffee has turned from the blue of the cleaner to an unpleasant green, having chemically scoured out the dregs and stains of a day's worth of coffee making from the steel tubes. He ducks out of the corral, heading for the kitchen door to retrieve the mop bucket to empty the percolator into.

"If you see Liz, you send her back up here, unless she's making eggs or something, then let her be, but tell her to make a couple more. The ol' stomach's really growlin'," Dark Suit says. "Even better if she found the steaks, bloody rare, remind her." Jimmy nods, noting how Light Suit looks up suddenly when Dark Suit mentions blood.

An idea strikes Jimmy, a way to get rid of Red Dress'… Liz's body… Bloody steaks, indeed. But if he cooked her up and fed her to Dark Suit… He'd never be able to feed him all of her, even if he shared her around to the others… Still, the thought hangs with him as he retrieves the mop bucket and wheels it back to the front.

Pushing open the door, the first thing Jimmy sees is Light Suit laying across the counter, being pummeled by Dark Suit. Their hats are gone. Their hair sticks out at odd angles. Dark Suit hauls back to strike Light Suit again, and Jimmy grabs a block-like steel napkin dispenser, launching himself over the counter with the help of a stool which spins and wobbles wildly behind him as he slides across the polished wood and drops to his feet on the other side, bringing the metal box down over Dark Suit's head. The man collapses, sliding backward onto the floor.

The other growls, a deep, guttural thing like a creature unto itself, racing from his throat and wrapping itself around them all. Jimmy's flesh crawls. He backs away as the man, eyes as wild as the howl that follows his growl, rolls over and rakes the countertop with ragged nails.

"Now see here-" Linen Suit protests. "There are ladies… present?" Light Suit turns on him, launching forward and bowling him over. They both vanish from Jimmy's sight behind the counter, but blood leaps back into view a moment later, spraying across the plate glass window of the storefront, the doors, the tiny brass bell. Navy Dress screams, backs straight over the back of the booth into view, then slips and falls backward, striking the table with the back of her head. A solid *thunk*! sound issues and she flows, practically liquid, over the bench seat and onto the floor beneath the table.

A tearing sound. A cracking, crunching sound. Linen Suit's hatless head flies up toward the door, spidering it with the impact before falling down, eyes wide, features twisted into a rictus of surprise and pain. Uncertain what to do, Jimmy ducks behind the counter as Light Suit rises to a hunched stance, sniffing around.

More crunching issues from what seems like a different direction… Dark Suit? Jimmy had thought it was his night to let go, but Light Suit is showing him up. From his hiding spot, Jimmy can see out into the night sky. The glare of the city lights blurs out the stars, but a full moon hangs just over the towering buildings. A sinking feeling fills his stomach as Light Suit leaps up onto the counter and focuses on him, growling.

Unarmed, Jimmy does the only thing he can think of: he pitches to the side and kicks against the far wall, launching himself through the space beneath the flip-up section of counter. He slides across linoleum redolent with pine-cleaner and scrambles across the gap to the kitchen door, where he pulls himself up and scans around for anything to defend himself with.

The room, lined with stainless steel stoves and vents on one side, similarly shiny coolers and freezer doors on the other, and piles of pots and pans and knives between seemed like a gauntlet of dangers during the day, with chef and waitstaff bustling about, knives chopping vegetables, cutting meat, mincing things. Now, it seemed like a desolate cave full of reflective surfaces ready to betray him.

The door swings open so violently, the breeze almost shoves Jimmy off his feet, and the panel strikes a prep table, laying over its metal corner with a crack and pop of stripping screws. The door clatters to the floor as Light Suit, now bloody and torn suit, growls again and swipes at him with nails that rake his flesh through the uniform shirt. The pain spurs him into action.

Jimmy runs around the side of the central chopping table, leaping over the pool of blood and skidding to a stop near the end of the table, grabbing up a knife in each hand. Light Suit charges for him, slipping on the fallen aprons and the blood beneath, bouncing off the coolers, then back to the heavy table on the other side before falling onto his back. Taking his moment, Jimmy lunges in, stabbing at Light Suit's belly. Flailing legs deflect his attack, knocking him into the cooler.

"You come in here, day in, day out, demanding, demeaning, destroying my self-worth, and for what? Some lousy coffee and stale pie? And now this? This?!" Jimmy says, nearly growling himself as Light Suit struggles to rise, shoes slipping in the blood. With a roar, he knocks his shoes off on a shelf under the table and tears away gray socks with satisfying ripping sounds. Knowing he's almost out of time, Jimmy slashes at hands and feet while retreating as Light Suit finally gets

The crazed aggressor shoves the table, tearing it from the bolts keeping it on the floor and toppling it toward the stove. Fire? Jimmy thought? Everything hates fire, especially wild beasts. Do werewolves care about fire? Before he can formulate a plan, claws rake across his chest, tearing one side of the shirt open. Buttons ping off hanging pots and onto the tile floor. Blood oozes down over his belly.

No! No! This is my night! Jimmy yells in his head, anger breaking the connection between his brain and his mouth. He turns the knives over to stab downward at Light Suit and lunges, blades plunging down into the space behind the other's clavicles. Cloth tears, then flesh. Blood spurts again, showering Jimmy. He hauls down, hearing one satisfying crack of bone as Light Suit grunts and dips on that side, while on the other, the metal snaps, leaving most of the blade in place as the stub slashes across Light Suit's chest, ripping away suit, shirt, and more flesh.

Light Suit growls and barrels into Jimmy, knocking him backward into the back wall of the kitchen. At the far end of the room, someone yells, commanding, but Jimmy's head swims and black consumes him consciousness.

Jimmy wakes to someone leaning over him.

"There he is!" A haunted face trying to smile for him says. "You're lucky, kid, this guy was a complete wacko. Everyone else is dead. We're going to need you to help us out with a sketch artist, if you can."

"Jees, Dan, give the kid a minute. He just fought off a serial killer," someone Jimmy can't see says.

"You didn't catch him?" Jimmy's eyes widen.

"Nah, we shot the Hell out of him. Even if he was a *real* werewolf instead of a sicko, he's seen his last full moon. We were hoping you could help us come up with good pictures of the victims, try to identify them, you know? Any names you might have caught would be helpful, too. Looks like two adult males, one teen girl and a woman we found in the freezer. They're… well, they're not pretty. Helluva night, huh?"

"Yeah… helluva night, officer. Helluva night."

Jimmy's wounds had been moderate, but after a few weeks in the hospital, he was released and is back on the job. The night is temperate, and it's early enough that people still stride the street in groups on the way to and from the theater and other venues.

Tick. The diner is busy, the cooks still clanging and sizzling away. Tock. Jimmy's been feeling itchy all day. Tick. The feeling has grown as night set in. Tock.

The moon peeks over nearby buildings, large, round, mesmerizing.

A sneer crawls across his face, chased by a growl that evolves to a howl.

PAS DE DOULER

200mF

ET LES DOUX HERITERONT

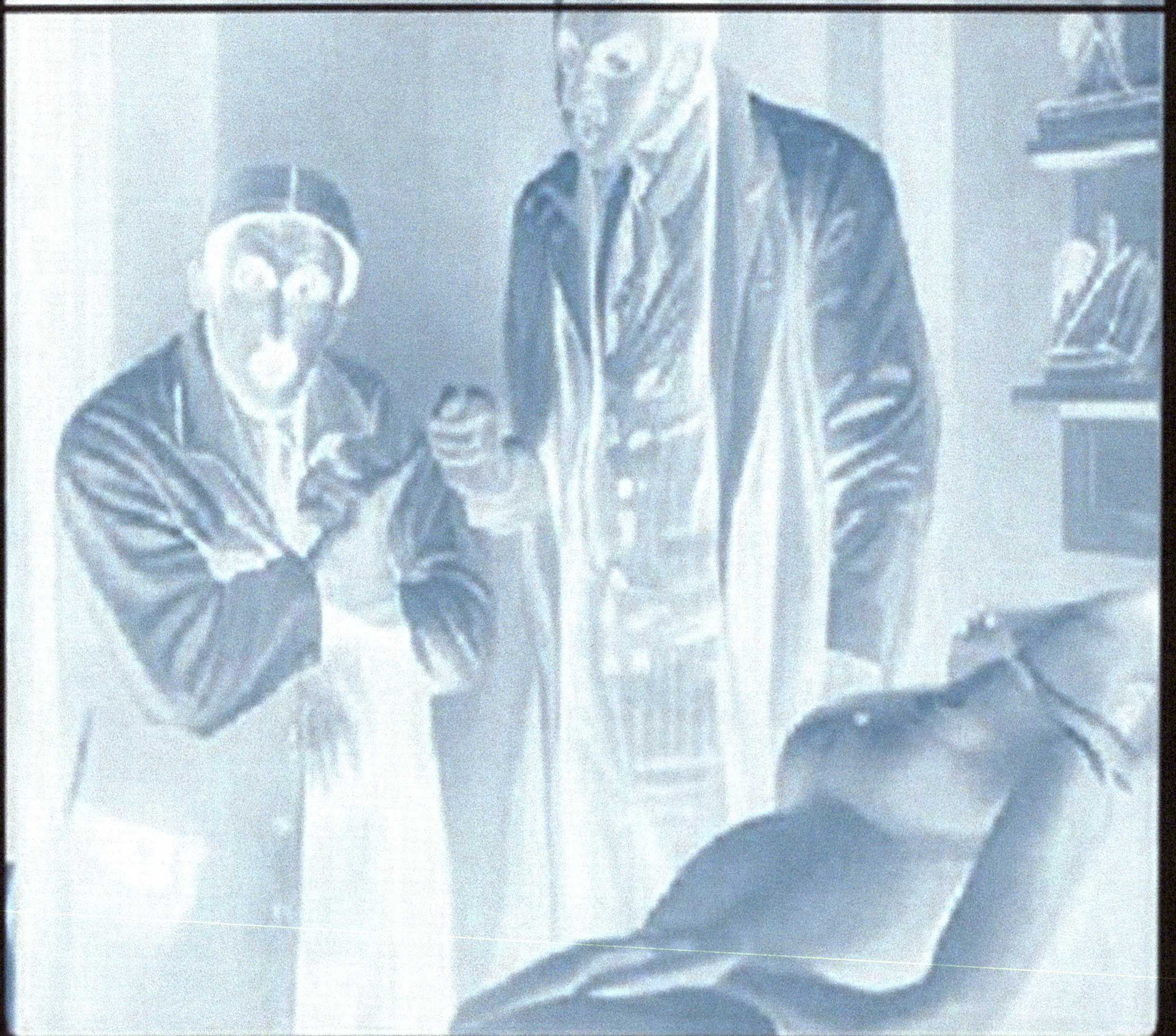

THÉATRE DU

GRAND GUIGNOL

20bis Rue Chaptal

Acte Un.

Hey, friend. Don't be afraid. There's still a human being inside, despite what you're seeing. Let me…let me just explain. Maybe you'll do me the favor of mercy – rather than just calling the cops. Give me anything but this life I have now. Give me blood, give me fire, give me a slit throat, but anything is better than living the life I live.

I would kill just to feel something. As you've seen, I have.

Allow me to elaborate, friend.

It was about a year ago, when I was living in the shittiest of streets in the biggest shithole on the planet, curling up with whatever I could cover myself with at night just to keep from freezing to death. Occasionally, I could sneak into one of the homeless shelters in town, but once they know you have a habit, you're almost always kicked right the fuck back out. I wasn't giving up the only thing that made me feel decent, so back on the streets I went.

Every now and then, this so-called "Christian mission" would come through, offering food and shelter to whoever would go with them to pray and shit, and every time, some of the street people would go with them, and we'd never see them again. Yeah, it was pretty fuckin' sus, but for a lot of us out on the streets, sus was the best we could hope for. Nobody was going to give us a fair deal. Everybody always wanted something. "There's always a price," my asshole dad always liked to say, "and everybody always pays."

Well, when the junk wrecked me bad enough where I couldn't get money for selling myself anymore, the supply of it ran dry and left me even worse off than I was. Not only was I broke, starving, and homeless, I was also going through withdrawal. I laid down in the street for what was intended to be the last time. Planning to die there, becoming just another statistic.

At least, that was the plan, until the Priest came along. Now, I think it's important to note that this dude was not really a priest. He had this presence about him that reminded me a lot of a priest, and it was just easier for me to think of him that way. He had a name, but when I first became involved with him, I hadn't the slightest idea what it was. When he was first involved in my life, I was all kinds of fucked up, and I didn't think to make a mental note of anything. Anyway, the Priest came along and gave me an alternative.

Now, the Priest was a weird looking guy, not at all a trustworthy looking person. He was tall, thin, reedy, and gaunt, like someone had drained the life force out of a six-foot-tall man. He had a hacking cough that seemed to bring up tiny droplets of blood with it, staining his handkerchief. His eyes were sunk deep into his head, and almost seemed to glow like hot cinders in the shadowy recesses of their sockets. His hair was scraggly and white, and very thin on top, but long enough to reach his shoulders. He looked frail, but there was something about him, some invisible quality, that just warned you not to fuck with this guy. He was serious business, and you should treat him like he was serious business.

The Priest was the one that found me first and called over the others that were with him. He coughed loudly into his handkerchief as the two other people, one man and one woman, worked to keep me from dying. They gave me a shot of something, some weird green liquid, and within seconds all of my withdrawal symptoms seemed to vanish. I didn't know what it was that they gave me, and at the time I didn't care. All I knew was that the pain stopped. That's all that mattered.

The Doctor, the man that gave me the shot of the weird green stuff, pulled me to my feet, and to my surprise, I didn't have any weakness in my limbs. I was able to stand like a completely healthy person, not like someone who'd been hooked on smack for years. My head was clear and there was no pain. Though I am not really accustomed to displays of emotion, tears welled up in my eyes, tears of gratitude for these strangers who took away the pain. The woman, who I quickly began calling the Future Girlfriend (had you seen her, you would understand), handed me a tissue, with which I quickly wiped away the offending tears.

The Priest smiled at me, but it was a smile that chilled me to the bone, a smile with bloodstained teeth. He said nothing, but instead let the Doctor and the Future Girlfriend do all the talking. They told me about their new street outreach program, that required actually very little on my part. All I had to do was attend their discussion group once a week, and they would provide food, shelter, and medical care to me at no cost. I mean, that's a better deal than most people with jobs and families get, right? It would have been stupid to say no, so I accepted their offer.

They put me on this truck with a few other gutter rats that all looked like they'd been scraped off of the bottom of someone's shoe, just like me, and took us to what they called the Processing Center. They gave me a chance to shower and change clothes into something clean and comfortable, if not exactly *haute couture*, and a full meal of pasta with red sauce and bread on the side. I wolfed that shit down like you wouldn't believe. It was more food at one sitting than I'd had in years. I was trying hard to find the downside to the deal, because even though I was off the street and had a full stomach, that innate pessimism is always there. You always wonder when it's all going to go to hell.

We were taken to individual rooms, with spartan, though comfortable, furnishings. I wasn't interested in reading or any of that shit. I just wanted to crash the fuck out, so I hopped in the twin-size bed and fell asleep almost immediately. I hadn't known a real bed for so long, I'd almost forgotten what one felt like. The sheets were soft and smooth and felt cool against my skin. I couldn't believe it, but I was comfortable, safe, and best of all, in no pain.

The next morning, Future Girlfriend came to visit me before breakfast, offering me a hot cup of coffee. F.G. was a very attractive young woman, probably near to my age, with dishwater blonde hair and just enough freckles to be cute. Her voice was slightly lower than you'd expect for a woman, but I didn't find it off-putting. Her smile was the kind that could catch the attention of a whole room full of people. One time, I even caught the Priest looking enamored by her smile. Suffice to say, I had no defense against it.

I took cautious sips from the steaming cup as we walked around the facility. Everything was so different from what I was used to. Everything was clean, orderly, and had almost no scent whatsoever. Where I was used to run-down brick and concrete, there was now glass, plastic, and metal. Everything was clean and white inside the facility, from the hallways right down to my bedding. F.G. explained that their methodology in rehabilitation was to immediately reintroduce people to clean environments, reinforcing the importance of being sanitary. Personally, I just liked not smelling like shit, puke, and week-old cheap booze. They could call it whatever the hell they wanted.

F.G. took me by the Medical Clinic next, for another shot of the green stuff. Again, I didn't think much of it at the time because it kept the withdrawal symptoms from appearing. I felt pretty good after every injection of the drug, which F.G. called Rathazine. The Doctor did a full physical on me, and pronounced me in surprisingly good health, considering the severe malnutrition, the years of smack addiction, and having the shit beaten out of me on more than one occasion by unsavory clientele. He said that I should continue weekly injections of Rathazine while I was still in the program, and arrangements could be made later on if I needed to continue treatment after leaving the program.

F.G. led me to the cafeteria for breakfast, which was a delicious mushroom omelet, wheat toast with apple butter, orange juice, and more coffee. It didn't stand a chance against me and was consumed within minutes. The dishes were taken away and F.G. returned shortly after to take me for a walk outside.

I'd be lying to you if I said I wasn't attracted to F.G. I mean, it's right in the name. The best times I had in the program were when it was just F.G. and I spending time together, even though she did everything she could to keep a professional detachment. I knew there was zero chance of a hook-up, but I didn't really care. It was just nice being treated like a worthwhile human being for once, you know? F.G. treated me like I was more than just some dying lump of flesh to be ignored, robbed, or violated.

I'm digressing again. You'll have to forgive me, but the closest I come to feeling anything these days are my memories of F.G. She meant a lot to me, even after what would come.

Anyway, we went for a walk outside, and F.G. told me all about the scope of the project, how the organization running the project had facilities in thirty-five cities around the world, working hard to clean up the streets and the people on them, turning lives around and giving people like me a new lease on life. All of this done with minimal commitment on the part of the participant, beyond the discussion group once a week. No forced religion, no political agenda, just people trying to help people.

I had been there for a couple days before my first discussion group. F.G. and the other staff members herded everyone into the main conference room, a spacious room with a massive table in the middle, surrounded by comfortable chairs. Everyone was escorted to one and seated. I settled in comfortably as the rest of the participants sat down with varying degrees of skepticism. After a moment or two, the Priest entered the room, sitting down at the head of the table and opening a thick binder to the first page, his eyes scanning the room. He introduced himself as Mr. Dargaard and began to explain the reason for the existence of the program, which he called New Dawn. Now, I don't necessarily mind having a catchy name for your homeless rehab program, but don't make it quite so culty if you don't want people's internal alarms to go off, you follow me? "New Dawn" sounds like the kind of thing that ends with everyone dead in tennis shoes and track suits trying to hitch a ride with a fucking UFO. Still, New Dawn had done a lot for me in a short period of time, and even though Dargaard scared me a little, F.G. and the Doctor seemed like decent enough people. Dargaard was very clear on the fact that we could leave New Dawn at any time we wished, which considerably eased people's minds. We could have whatever contact with the outside world we wished and could have visitors at the facility during set visiting hours. New Dawn was not a prison, neither was it an institution. We were not inmates and should not have to live like inmates.

After Dargaard's explanation, I felt considerably better about New Dawn and about my presence there. Several of the other participants also felt far more confident in the program, now that they knew they had freedom to do what they wished. The one hard and fast rule at New Dawn, was no drugs whatsoever, and I was fine with it. The Rathazine seemed to alleviate my cravings for the heroin anyway, so it wasn't that hard a rule to obey. Others didn't care so much for the rule, and left New Dawn, no questions asked. Dargaard didn't stop them.

It seemed that New Dawn practiced what they preached, and my confidence in them grew.

My first full week at New Dawn passed uneventfully, keeping myself busy with educational programs. I learned how to use a computer for something other than looking for porn, drugs, or hook-ups.

I dipped my toes into the water of business software and basic robotics, making a very basic robotic arm do silly tricks. F.G. was delighted at my progress, but I felt like I should be doing more with this second chance. I felt as if maybe I could contribute a little back to the program that had literally saved my life.

F.G. listened as I explained my desire, and nodded her head accordingly, but explained after that the New Dawn center was already staffed to capacity, but if I really wanted to help, Mr. Dargaard had a project that I could perhaps help with, if I was interested. In my zeal and naivete, I said that I was more than interested. She smiled and clapped me on the shoulder, saying that I was what New Dawn was all about.

When F.G. presented me to Dargaard as a candidate for his project, at first, he rejected me, saying that I was too soon off the streets, too recently introduced to rathazine. She made a passionate plea to the older man, but he just would not allow it. He said, however, that he would keep me in mind in the future, once I had been part of New Dawn a little longer and had some time to get the streets out of my blood.

I was crushed. I lay in my bed that night, unable to sleep. I just kept trying to figure out why I wasn't good enough. I'd been the model participant, throwing myself into everything that New Dawn offered me, and yet Dargaard seemed to think I was too tainted by the streets.

I redoubled my efforts. I did everything that was expected of me and then some. No one kept their room as clean as mine. No one was as disciplined as I was about being on time to activities. No one was as timely about their weekly rathazine shot as I was. You could set a clock by me. I was a complete chatterbox in discussion groups, spilling my guts when it was appropriate, letting others talk when they had things to say. I wanted to be the absolute poster child for New Dawn.

I had to be. I had to be good enough for Dargaard.

Acte Deux.

Sure enough, I became the embodiment of what New Dawn stood for. I was the junkie-turned-productive-member-of-society that New Dawn wanted everyone to see, and they showed me off like I was an Italian car or painting or some shit like that.

F.G. paraded me around town, putting me on the local news, making New Dawn a household name. Making my name synonymous with New Dawn and with its mission.

Dargaard didn't care or didn't seem to notice if he did. I wanted to put my immaculately clean fist through my brilliantly white wall. Instead of doing that, though, I decided after about six months in the program that it was time for me to start planning to check out. I needed to find a place to live, find a job, get some money together, get basic supplies like clothing and food. There was just so much to think about, things I hadn't thought about when I was on the street. F.G. was so incredibly helpful during that time. She helped me find a decent apartment, get a job that didn't involve being elbow-deep in hamburger grease, even pick out a few outfits that were both professional and decent-looking. New Dawn covered my medical expenses and paid my bills for the first two months whileon my own. It really felt like everything was going to work out for the best.

Then it really started on a rainy night in October, when the temperature dipped into the forties, and I was snuggled up on my couch with my warm blanket and my favorite plushie. I was watching some mindless show and getting ready to go to bed early, as I tended to do on work nights, when there was a knock on the door. Now, I didn't get a lot of visitors. I didn't really know anyone outside of New Dawn, and I felt it was best to kind of close the book on that part of my life. I had no idea who could have been outside my door, so I peeked through the peephole. I was shocked, to say the least, to see Dargaard standing there, his expression as sour as ever.

Completely disregarding my newly regained voice of intuition, I invited him in. He didn't say anything as he entered, only nodding politely as he passed by me. Once I shut the door behind him, he actually spoke. He told me that the time – my time - had come, as I'd proven myself to be reliable, driven, and most of all, stable. I wasn't sure what that was supposed to mean at the time, but I took it as a compliment. He held out a small card to me, which I took, and told me that I should report to that address the next day for work. I, of course, explained to him that I already had a job. He merely grinned, a thin, crooked, disturbing grin, and said that it was taken care of already.

The following morning, I went to the address on the card, and found what looked like a large medical building. I went inside and was greeted by a woman at a large reception desk. She took the card from me, and picked up the nearby phone, mumbled something into it, and informed me that someone would be with me shortly. I looked to the right of the reception desk, and saw a large, solid-looking metal door with a keypad next to it. As this looked to be the only way into the rest of the building, I had to wonder why such security was necessary. Who were they trying to keep out, exactly?

A man came out of the door after a moment and ushered me into the back of the building. There was only an elevator there, which I was shown into. The door closed behind me, and suddenly I was filled with a feeling of dread. Something was very wrong here, something that requires a ridiculous amount of security. When the doors opened, my dread only increased, because there were what appeared to be armed guards posted up and down the hallway. There was also another man, one in a lab coat, who was smiling broadly at me as I slowly stepped out of the elevator. He approached me, his hand extended in a friendly manner.

He introduced himself as Dr. Nsabimana, one of the heads of the project. He wanted to put me at ease, since Dargaard rarely ever did such a thing. All that was to happen that day was two injections, one of Rathazine and one of a very small dose of what they referred to as an experimental pain killer. I was to be tested for reactions to the pain medication, and if there was, I would be disqualified from further participation in this part of the project, though I would still have employment. He told me I was going to have a job no matter what, so I should just relax and enjoy the easy part.

Now, I did find it odd that I spent months getting off smack only for the very same people who helped me kick the habit to now shoot me up with other shit. Still, Dr. Nsabimana swore that it was all safe and fine for me to do, so I agreed. He showed me into a room with one of those weird dentist chairs that he had me sit in, and he leaned it back to where I'm almost lying flat. He filled a syringe with rathazine. In the dim light I could have sworn that shit almost glowed.

That needle went into my arm, and as the green fluid flowed into me, I felt a warm sensation come over me that I'd never felt before, a sensation of safety, of peace. It was nice, not a feeling I was used to when having something injected into me.

Then came the second needle, and though I didn't know what exactly it was or what the dosage might have been, whatever it was hit me like a truck. It was like when I was a kid and I'd swipe my mom's Seroquel. it was that kind of almost paralyzed feeling, where gravity suddenly feels a hundred times stronger, and all you want to do is sleep. It wasn't unpleasant, but if this was a tiny dose, I'd hate to imagine what a strong dose would be like. I struggled to stay awake, but sleep claimed me after what could only have been minutes.

I awoke sometime later, and Dr. Nsabimana entered the room, broad smile affixed in place. He told me that I'd had no reaction to the drugs, and that everything went exactly as it had supposed to have. He then told me that I had been asleep for just over seven hours, and because I was out that long that I shouldn't feel any lingering aftereffects. He also informed me that I was good to move on to Phase Two. Of course, I had no idea what hell Phase Two was. I hadn't even *heard* of Phase Two. It was the first time I felt afraid since I'd joined New Dawn.

Acte Trois.

I was told to report back to the facility in a week and given a paycheck for fucking eight thousand dollars. I felt like I was on top of the world. I had money, I had free time, I had work, I had a place of my own, everything was looking up.

Phase Two was a lot of the same, though there were some exceptions. I'd taken to wearing a watch, just out of curiosity, and there were some episodes of lost time where there was a disparity between the time that passed and the time that Dr. Nsabimana said had passed. There was a space of almost four hours that I couldn't account for, and that is a large amount of time, during which just about anything could have happened.

Apart from the missing time, I didn't have any other reason to think there was anything to worry about, but something still gnawed at me. Something I couldn't put my finger on, something just outside of my notice, but it was there, lurking. I was basically getting paid to sleep, but something was just not right about it.

Then came Phase Three. Instead of just laying on a chair getting buzzed out of my skull all day, I was receiving large amounts of rathazine with unknown drugs mixed in, and then put in front of a computer and asked to perform certain tasks, tasks like controlling a simple robotic arm, much like the one I'd played around with at New Dawn or play odd games where I'd have to choose the right picture before time ran out. Nothing too suspicious, but nothing at all like in Phase Two. I was expected to be awake and alert the entire time, and if I were to fail at a task, I would have to start that section again until it was mastered.

It was hard work and when I would finally head home at the end of the day, I was exhausted. Still, the paychecks increased accordingly, and they kept me coming.

After a couple weeks of Phase Three, Dr. Nsabimana announced that I was ready to move into Phase Four, but there were going to be some changes necessary. I would have to remain at the facility during Phase Four and higher due to the high security level of the project, but quarters would be provided that were comfortable and spacious, on par with my apartment. They would also send someone to fetch some of my personal belongings, if I felt I needed to have some of my things with me. I insisted someone bring my blanket and my favorite plushie. It felt odd, a grown adult asking for their plushie, but we all have our creature comforts.

On my first day of Phase Four, I was shown to my new quarters, on the top floor of the facility. It was a nice-sized apartment, close to the size of mine in the city. I was told to change into what looked like surgical scrubs and take the elevator to the seventh floor and await instructions. I did so, and eventually a short, bearded man dressed like me came out of the elevator and flashed me a smile. He explained that as part of Phase Four, he was going to install some sort of implant into my arm that would allow more efficient dosage of the necessary chemicals. I was taken back for a moment because I sure as hell didn't want to have anything implanted in my body, and no one had said anything about surgery being part of the deal.

This doctor, Dr. Stanton, was very persuasive, however, and managed to talk me into accepting. The procedure took about an hour, and I was awake through the entire process.

It was quite interesting, watching Dr. Stanton open up a part of my arm, and reroute some of the larger blood vessels through the implant. What was even more interesting, however, was how the implant itself almost seemed to grow into my arm, to become a part of me. I chalked it up to the anesthetic because there's no such thing as an implant that fuses itself into your body, of course.

Dr. Stanton hooked up three lines to the new implant, though I am to this day not sure what they all were. I'm pretty sure one was rathazine. They loved that stuff and used it all the time. I'm still not sure what it does, apart from shutting down withdrawal symptoms. The second and third, I can only guess, because once they started the flow, it was as if I ceased to exist. Everything just shut off and went black.

An instant later, I opened my eyes, and found myself in my new bed, with Dr. Stanton standing over me. He was smiling, saying that everything had gone fine, and that I had just had a stronger reaction to the new cocktail than expected. He did not think there was anything to worry about going forward, but he did recommend that I get some rest. He left my quarters, and I sat up in bed. I looked down at the new machine that stuck just slightly out of my arm and gave it a slight nudge with my finger. There was no give. It was anchored deep in the tissue of the arm. It hurt like hell when I touched it. I mean it hurt more than it should have, considering that there was no inflammation around the implant site, and everything looked healed and healthy. Nothing hurt until I touched it.

What was this thing?

The next morning came, and I was instructed to report back to the seventh floor. Dr. Stanton was waiting for me this time, with a grim look on his face. He explained that something had gone wrong with the implant during the night, and that he would have to repair it. It would not involve any pain on my part, but he would have to render me unconscious while he worked on it. Remembering the pain that I had felt the previous night after touching the device, it sounded feasible to me, so I consented to the procedure.

I opened my eyes afterwards, and the look on Dr. Stanton's face was far less grim. He informed me that the procedure had gone well, but they were going to have to keep me in the infirmary overnight for observation. There was some, as he put it, anomalous activity in the implant and they wanted to make sure everything was working right

It was around this time that I started questioning just what in the hell was going on, though I'll admit I should have started questioning sooner. My loyalty to Dargaard and to New Dawn, which felt like centuries ago at this point, was driving me to stay – but my survival instinct and my desire to not be a guinea pig felt otherwise.
They said:
"GET THE FUCK OUT OF HERE, NOW."

Acte Final.

I laid there in the infirmary, on a cold, uncomfortable hospital bed, tubes connected to the weird device attached to my arm, pumping God-alone-knows-what into my body, and I felt like a fucking idiot. Sleep came, but only fitfully, interrupted occasionally by the incessant beeping of the monitors hooked up to me, monitors measuring God-only-knows-what.

I was woken unceremoniously during one of my brief interludes of sleep by strong hands holding me down and fastening restraints around my wrists and ankles. Fear grabbed hold of me quickly, and I struggled to no avail against the restraints and the strong men who held me in place, men whose faces I could not see. Dr. Stanton came into the room, carrying what looked like a toolbox. He set it down and opened it, pulling out some sort of pneumatic gun and a large vial of some chemical that he attached to the gun. He pressed the it against my left arm, and I heard the quick snap of the gun being fired, followed by a jolt of pain. Then my world started to get a little out of focus, as if everything was just slightly out of phase with itself. He said to the larger men that I won't be a concern any longer and dismissed them.

He connected several tubes to the implant on my arm and started some chemicals flowing into it, and into me. The world got stranger still, and I could have sworn that I was hallucinating at that point. I was seeing things that were not, could not, be there. Wrong things. Things that defy description. Things that wait for us just beyond the barrier of wakefulness. Then he told me it's time for Phase Five and left the room. Someone else came in and everything changed.

I do not know who the person was that entered the room, only that once she did, it was like every neuron in my brain began to burn. It felt like someone held my very mind in their hand and decided to crush it with all their might. I know I screamed, but I don't know for how long. The woman just looked at me and smiled. She knew that my mind was melting. She knew that something was tearing my consciousness apart from within and it was precisely what she wanted to happen. y.

I fell to the ground shortly after that, and I wish I could tell you that everything skips from there to here, but it doesn't. No, I wasn't so lucky.

I came to at some point later, and I was strapped to an operating table. People in full hazmat gear were standing all around me, pointing at various parts of my body, muttering to each other just under my ability to hear. I was pretty sure Dr. Stanton was one of them, but in the hazmat suit it was hard to tell one person from another, even with him being a short little shit. They were working on me, this much I knew, but oddly I felt no pain, no pain at all. I could feel the movement of probes and sutures within my flesh, but there was no pain. I felt the sensation of tissue rending as the scalpel slid cleanly through, but it didn't hurt.

I felt panic well up within my mind for an instant, but something, some arcane mechanism somewhere, suppressed it. All that remained was curiosity, curiosity as to what exactly was being done to my body.

It was then, at that moment, that I saw something that I will never forget, and something that you will do me the mercy of taking from me if you're as fast on the trigger as you seem to think you are. I turned my head just slightly to the left, as far as I was able to in my restrained state and caught a glimpse of another group of people in the same hazmat suits standing not far from the operating table where I lay splayed open. One of them turned to face where we were, holding something that I still can't identify. It looked alive, but I will be goddamned if it was from Earth. It was grotesque, a bizarre little organ in a shade of blue I didn't think nature was capable of producing. It pulsated and writhed in a way that unsettled me, and it unsettled me even more that the man holding this unsavory thing was approaching me. He handed the foul organ to one of the doctors working on me, and they placed it within my abdomen, saying something about how the new organ would metabolize a hundred times more efficiently than the digestive system I wouldn't even miss.

Over the span of two hours, the process repeated. Parts of me would be removed, and parts of…something…would be put into their place.

All throughout this process, the incessant humming of the pumps could be heard, the pumps that kept strange ichors flowing through the implant in my arm and into this new thing I had for a body The scientists and doctors working on and around me never spoke above a loud mumble, so I knew precious little of what was happening.

I do know that I saw the woman standing outside of the operating theater. She was watching it all happen. I don't know who she is, but I know that she is at the very heart of their operation. It all goes back to her. If only I could remember more about her face, her appearance, anything that could tell me who she is, but trying to remember anything is like hitting a wall. But it doesn't hurt. Nothing hurts. Nothing delights me, nothing saddens me, nothing feels like anything.

I cannot feel anything but fear and hatred anymore. She stole everything else from me.

But I feel no pain.

No pain.

So do it. End me. Free me from the grip of the monster that owns me. There won't be any pain. Pull the trigger and end me.

Do it before she makes me do it to you.

Mlle en morceau

les....meres....peuvent....etre....l'enfer

THÉATRE DU

GRAND GUIGNOL

20bis Rue Chaptal

Mum died three weeks ago. Her doctor listed "Multiple dislocations of cervical vertebrae; partial asphyxiation" as the cause on her death certificate. He even explained the big words to me like I was a twelve-year-old as he sat behind his ridiculously large, stained oak desk. Mum probably would have done the same thing, explain something she knew I understood to me, albeit without the desk and the medical credentials.

"Your mother likely lost consciousness before she passed and while it was likely a less than peaceful, it happened quickly. We don't like to list asphyxiation first on the certificate, ma'am. It being a…"

"Suicide?"

"Well, yes," the doctor answered. I handed the documentation back to him, like a baton in a relay race. Was his manipulation of the paperwork supposed to be a small blessing? I knew what happened. The carotid arteries in her neck were blocked, depriving the brain of oxygen. Once her airway closed, breathing was impossible. She didn't break her neck, but she sure fucked it up good – but not so much as to actually kill her. What did it matter? Whatever.

I, on the other hand, would call it a prolonged bout with severe depression, and everything that comes with such an extended period of mental illness. And when I say prolonged, I mean her entire life. And by everything, I mostly mean the mania days, minute to minute mood swings, and the weeks of anhedonia. Her cycles came in ebbs and flows and never in any kind of patterns that could predicted. The last two years had been especially horrible. It was a dark period for both her and me, leading up to her recent *coup de grâce*. For me, it led to her Pockabook.

Freckled onto the shell of chaos that held her life within were the two or three friends she had, or thought she had - but the lack of any more than those few made countless blemishes that overshadowed everything. The presence of the former made her better, but absences of the latter made her far, far worse. Mum could never keep a real friend, and she did try. Well, she did sometimes. She'd try until she'd conclude that she didn't want anyone around her no matter how good they were to her..

That left me as the only real constant presence in her life, and for the past two years, I lived with her as a constant caregiver. At best, I had mixed feelings about this arrangement. It went like this: When Mum was manic, she could be fun. We'd pick up and take a drive to the seashore and get ice cream cones.

But the fun would end when she inevitably took a roller coaster dive into the valley of despondency. Our trips never ended well. Now that she was gone, there weren't going to be anymore of those journeys. No more ice cream. People came by the house, wished me well, and kept me fed for the first couple of weeks after I moved in with her. Then they disappeared as if taken by rapture.

So, I disappeared too, eventually. Two years later, to be exact. Can you already see where this is going? Sure you can. Two years later I took a mental health break. Self-care I guess is what it's called now. _I went to a friend's house for a weekend. She died the first night I wasn't home keeping watch over her. Was it my presence that kept her going? I doubt the woman could truly care about anyone that much. Was she trying to punish me? Again, I don't she cared that much to have that level of desire for revenge. She was just waiting for her opportunity.

The funeral was yesterday afternoon, and all I could think during the ceremony about what I'd do afterwards – I kept seeing myself covetously enjoying the last of Auntie's meatloaf, while watching Wheel of Fortune on the couch. Without Mum.

I felt numb, a spectator to my own life. I'd wept for the week between when I found her the morning I returned home and yesterday. She was hanging from a belt in the bathroom, slung over the shower curtain rod. That's not usually an option for anyone weighing more than hundred and ten or so pounds, but Mum was a smoker, not an eater. Food was always optional.

The coroner put her time of death just after midnight.

She'd carried it out hours after I'd left for my friends' place.

Eyes slightly open, the blood vessels erupted. Her ensanguined stare, irreverent despite my shock. Drool had fallen and dried within the few bristly hairs that called her chin home. Mum's neck was bent in a peculiar, questioning angle as if to ask me if I was truly surprised. Scratch marks engraved upon her neck expressed her self-doubt. Too little too late. I peered at her hands finding grated skin, blood and hair embedded in her fingernails. As the shock waned the smell hit me. A putrefied boiled dinner. Sweaty, rotten meat and cabbage heaped on sewage.

Amidst those tears during the week, I'd I constantly think *She's in a better place* - the start of a prayer that never had a second line and therefore never came to an end. Before I left that night – the one when she took her life - we fought about something I thought trivial at the time..

She'd started talking about making arrangements in case something to were to happen to her, just out of the blue. I brushed her off almost the second after she began speaking.

"You're just saying that to get me to not go to Kate's house, Mum. Not cool."

Then the argument ensued. I never thought the "something" she was referring to would ever be self-inflicted, much less happen hours later.

Talking about it now…I think maybe she did do it out of pure spite for me, rather than it being the final toll exacted by her illness.

Fucking Mum. The feeling's mutual.

Acte Deux.

Going through her personal effects would have been hard enough just on its own, after what I'd been through. There's so much more than just that task, however, when a loved one passes away. For some, it's the most difficult. I just didn't want to do it. This chore could have been prevented if I had just showed that I cared just that little bit more. If I hadn't assumed that this was just the way she was and everything would be fine, she'd still be here. I may as well have looped the belt on the shower curtain rod myself the second I walked out the door. But it's not the blaming myself aspect for her suicide happening that made it so hard to even start the chore.

Whenever I've gone into her room I could still smell "her", the *real* "Her" and not what I experienced when I'd found her strung up by a single strap of leather. Mum's unmistakable, characteristic aroma was made up of two scents: the intertwined odors of "Skin So Soft", that sickly sweet smelling body lotion that held a spot in every geriatric's bathroom closet, and the smell of tobacco from the cheapest cigarettes money could barely buy. I felt like if I disturbed anything in her room, her smell would kick up and whisper her name into my thoughts at first. It would then grow so powerful it would scream her name into the center of my brain after.

But it had to be done. Couldn't have it hanging over me, like her-

No dancing around the task. I went into her bedroom and straight for her closet.

First trip in, I grabbed the stuff on coat hangers. Wasn't much, so one trip was all it took to get the lot of it. I tossed all of it on her bed, which was still made.

On the second trip I grabbed everything off the upper shelf. There were a couple bankers' boxes filled with loose pictures.

. A pair of moccasins she never wore. She was afraid to fall down the stairs when she wore them, and the woman never went out unless she had to. And lastly, as if it had been waiting for me all along, her pocketbook. The Pockabook.

Mum was always weird about her pocketbook – most moms were in the 70s and 80s in fact. They all had them, and they were all big enough to hold half the planet in them. You're too young to know about what our moms were like back then.

Under no circumstance was I allowed to go through, let alone even touch her "pockabook". That wasn't a rule that was ever said out loud or stated, just one I was supposed to have just known. I didn't. I had to learn that fact the hard way. So, when I was nine, I rifled through this very bag to steal a few bucks for the ice cream truck, thinking I was ever so clever in thinking of and then doing the deed.

Of course, she caught me. And when she did, I saw her in a state so angry her convulsions from pure rage probably shook the earth up to a mile away. Up until that moment, I'd never seen her even so much as tremble – she was always so calm. Jaw clenched, green eyes burning with incensed fire, Mum snatched the Pockabook from my grasp with the ferocity of a meth junkie lighting a pipe. Once she'd taken her property back from my pawing hands, her bare hand came down as a pendulum would, whacking me one, two, three….ten times in a steady rhythm on my ass. My skin sang, surely, but I was wounded more so by the deafening silence that followed. When she was done, Mum simply stared at me.

There was no explanation for the physical violence. There was no need for one, either.

I'd learned to NEVER go through Mum's Pockabook.

When I pulled it from the shelf, the Pockabook was still as heavy as a full gallon of milk. Made mostly of leather, it was something she spent a fortune on in whichever bygone decade she'd first bought it. When I held the Pockabook now and ran my hands along its exterior all these years since Mum had owned the thing, the leather felt buttery. The color of it matched the way she took her coffee, light with cream. The gold paint on the zipper was all worn at the edges, exposing the plastic underneath.

I sat down on her bed and peeked into the pocket on the short side of the bag, using both index fingers to pry it open. As soon as I did, the smell/whisper/scream I'd dreaded before I came into the room made its appearance. Skin So Soft and old tobacco, just like I told you.

She'd caught me messing with the Pockabook yet again. I flinched, closed my eyes, and braced myself for a smack that would never come. When opened my eyes a few seconds later, then relaxing my shoulders and resuming my investigation, I laughed to myself. Nothing to be afraid of.

I found her matching cigarette holder, made of the same Mum approved, coffee-colored leather. It was one of those vaguely rectangular pouches with a clasp at the top that snapped in place like an "X". Inside, an obnoxious, orange Bic lighter had been wedged next to a soft pack of Camel Lights. Camel. She must have splurged the last time she'd reloaded the holder. Two stale butts were still inside. Their bittersweet perfume permeated the Pockabook.

The Pockabook already felt like a pre-meditated, twisted trap she'd left behind for me to find. I stopped for an instant, afraid to reveal anymore of Mum's secrets, for that exact reason.

Why was it so sacred to her? Why did I feel like I should have been looking for justification or maybe the reason why I hadn't been allowed to go into her Pockabook, other than just because it was 'hers'? Was it simply because she'd kept a never-ending stock of odds and ends, this and that, or whatever one might need should any number of situations arise during the day. Was it simply a totem, like a Rabbit's Foot or a lucky coin – a sink into which she dumped her anxiety when it became too much?

The perfect example of this was the EpiPen she'd kept in there – ostensibly in case a bee should decide to sting me. I had to chuckle, because the thought of that EpiPen junking around inside always reminded me of the carpet bag Mary Poppins carried around that was full of all the things you didn't know you needed.

"You can't very well fit this shit in your dungarees, can you?" Mum always said.

But I wasn't allergic to bees. I wasn't – am still not – allergic to anything. So can you guys please stop saying this is allergic reaction? Allergies don't cause people to lose limbs. Back to my story.

Probing around the cool, second skin of silk lining the inside of Pockabook, I felt for the zipper to the inner pocket. There, to the right, was the object of my latest search, already unzipped halfway. I opened it up all the way to reveal her checkbook with pen still attached and a half a roll of LifeSavers – Wintergreen, coil of aluminum foil wrapping intact. No EpiPen though. Maybe she'd realized she'd never need the thing.

Also in the inner pocket, folded in half, was a torn piece of lined paper with a handwritten list. I used to poke fun at how long it would take her to write anything out by hand. Thanks to the nuns at her Catholic elementary school, her traumatic memories of shame and stinging knuckles had conditioned her to always take her time and achieve that perfect 20-degree slant to her letters. I ran my thumb over her writing, feeling the depression made by the pen.

At last, it was time for the main event, the bight of bric-a-brac that made up the central pocket of the Pockabook. And what was inside, I guess, is what got me here with you.

Now pay attention because I'm only going go through this last part with you one more time.

Acte Trois.

The central pocket was filled to the top with so much shit, I thought it'd take me the rest of today just to sort through its contents.

First thing I found, on the top of that pile of mayhem were a couple of paperback Harlequin novels. Dull and uninspired pieces of literary garbage, both had Fabio in a suggestive position on the cover where he would seduce all who looked upon his countenance with that signature smolder. Gross. I guess Mum needed to get her rocks off somehow. After excising those two wastes of paper, I spied something metallic next to her wallet. Intrigued, I looked fleetingly over my shoulder and shoved my hand deeper into the bag to reveal the treasure Mum left behind. It was a vintage compact, darkened by years of neglect. In desperate need of a polish. I remember her telling me that it had belonged to Nana.

Never met my Nana. Only heard stories.

I opened it up to see that there was a grayish powder that covered much of the actual mirror as well as the inside of it. Mum had told me once that Nana died from an allergic reaction to the powder in this compact. Why on Earth would she want to keep it? So strange was its presence even without the back story – Mum, she never really wore make-up. Every once in a while she'd wear her trademark mauve lipstick but that was it. But the compact? She'd kept it, and likely never opened the thing up – ever – to use the mirror inside. I snickered. Maybe she's kept it as a kind of trophy, for outliving her own mother. Then I thought, maybe I should find my own trophy. Sure as hell wasn't going to be the belt she hung herself with though. Something from The Pockabook. Something of *hers*. I put my hand back in to see what else I could find.

"Fuck!." I exclaimed. I'd felt a small, violent jab in my hand. It was followed with a "Jesus, Mary, and fuckin' Joseph!" Yeah, I know what you're thinking. I'd never said it myself, but Mum always did. For whatever reason, that came out of me when it first bit me.

What the hell was that? I thought. I yanked out my hand to see a rivulet of blood starting in the heel of my palm and running down my forearm, already halfway to the elbow. Not wanting to make a mess of Mum's things, I put my palm to my mouth, pulling at the source of the bleeding until it felt like it had stopped. I pulled it away from my face, only to see that my hand began to turn a grayish blue. Once that extremity had completely changed to that corpse color, the decay began to work its way slowly down my arm as I watched. My heart pounding wildly, I reached inside the Pockabook to find little shit that stabbed me.

And then the world in front of me just…fractured. Best way I can describe it.

I thought I was having a panic attack, at least at first. I looked over at the Pockabook to catch the zipper pull look as if it had been tugged from the corner, all on its own – like it was trying to get unstuck from the leather. The pull was stuck. The elements on the sides of the zipper had been shaved into tooth-like razors, maintaining their faded, gold painted hue. The zipper pull wrenched free from the bag with a jerk. It fell to the bed, limp. The leather sighed, then shuddered…undulated as if the thing had somehow just grown a spine one vertebrae at a time. A brown ooze, something like a running, creamy vomit of wintergreen, cigarettes and curdled coffee, seeped out from between the two pieces of leather that were once connected by the zipper, which resembled a mouth more and more by the second. I gagged and held the full release back. My own sick collected at the back of my throat. Mum always told me to smile when I felt that "technicolor yawn coming on" – she was so fuckin' weird. I was in too much pain from the bite and the rot to smile, but I did just the same to spite her.

Smiling. The pain kept growing, along with the urge to vomit. The rot felt as if had reached my shoulder.

I was fuckin *smiling*. The pain was so great the room began to spin.

I held a mouthful of puke between my cheeks. Maybe the rot was in my brain, because I held my arm out toward the Pockabook.

Oh, *I WAS SMILING* at this fuckin Pockabook because I couldn't look anywhere else.

Everything I saw in there moments ago was gone; a second row of teeth wazz zipper all I could zee! Not zipper teeth! They were barbed, on each side. Dozens of tiny double-edged swordz were embedded in the pink zatin lining of the bag. Both rows of teeth zipperee zip pinched shut, crunching into my wrizt.

CRUNCH the teeth went! Rip my wrist into the mouth it go! Zip zipperowwww!

There was zoooo much blood - it gushed everywhere, slowly at first, all over Mum's baby blue, diamond tufted, chenille bedspread. I used to love lying on this bedspread as Mum read her Mary Higgins Clark books, breathing in Downy, feeling the occasional shake of the bed when Mum had a coughing fit. I felt calmed thinking about it.

"I'm fine, I'm fine, I'm fine," she'd say.

"I'm fine, I'm fine, I'm fine," I said zip ziperee. I was cauzing the bed to shake rocking back and forth, a geyser of blood spraying the walls, the carpet, some even hit the ceiling.

I looked down and saw a red gelatinous pulp, blood pudding, oozing over the sides of the bag. Then The Pudding lepppt at my stumpping. The Teeth then slowly chewed leftover sinew, reminding me of my brother eating greeeesy chicken wings. He always ate with his mouth open; Mum hated it. So did I, so did I, so did I.

I looked down into the Pockabook and spit my hand back at me and it landed flaccid, turned blue and bloody, staining the satin lining. The compact was still clutched within my dearly departed hand. My hand was sad because it had...

The compact was open still unbroken. A glint in the mirror caught my eye, only it wasn't reflecting anything back to me. It was crudely painted black. Watching as uniformed strangers flooded Mum's room, darkness fell around me.

"I'm sorry Mum! I'm sorry! I'll never doubt you again! I'll never disobey again! I'll never leave you!!"

And then I woke up, here. So you belieeeeve me, right?

Acte Final.

"So, you believe me, right? About Pockabook and The Pudding and The Teeth?" the woman in the back asked. She was directly out of her fucking mind.

"Yes ma'am. We believe you. Everything's under control," I told her, in the most half-assed reassurance I could offer and still sound like I actually gave a shit.

I turned to my partner and mouthed "*psycho*", like Adam Sandler did in *Happy Gilmore*. Should have known the kid wouldn't get the reference. He's in his friggin' twenties. I had to resist the urge to perform the universal sign for crazy – circular motion, finger pointed at a temple. Pockabook lady in back might start flailing against her four-point again.

The radio clicked to life. "Unit ten-bravo, come back." I picked up the receiver and responded.

"Ten-bravo, come back."

"Just looked through the medicine cabinet – Miss Wilson was on some serious anti-psychotics – quietapine, olanzapine, clozapine all current. Why was she prescribed an Epi-Pen knowing the reaction it would cause?"

"I'll call ahead to the hospital get a bed ready in the psych ward for her when we arrive." I said.

I hung up the receiver. The fuck was up with this lady and her mother anyway? I turned around and saw her smiling. And staring. Her look almost had me believing that her Mum's handbag had come to life and bit off her hand. I even looked down at her side - yep, still there. Not a scratch.

I looked back into her eyes. She said:

I told you I wasn't allergic.

GRAND

GOUGET, ORVAL, LERICHE, DENEVRY, ETC

GUIGNOL

La Preqelle de "*Bleed*" de Michael STRONG

Acte Un.

Rain. Darkness. Fog. Stinking cobblestones. Wet brick. Laughter distant enough to sound like screams drifted to his ears. Drunkards staggering on to their next stop, he supposed. Strange how overbearing the dark buildings and streets seemed after the shining light of Delhi. London had not changed in the decade Galloway spent in India and he hadn't missed it. The pending return to Delhi with his family couldn't come fast enough. He still dreamt of jasmine on the breeze as the smog polluted his lungs.

The last memory he had of this wretched city was an unpleasant one: his reprimand from London Hospital Medical College. Grave robbing, they cited him with, and threatened his expulsion. How did the bloody fools expect them to learn if there were no anatomical specimens upon which to practise their craft? But no matter. Doctor Galloway the senior came down from Edinburgh fast enough for sparks to fly from the carriage wheels, his dark eyes reflecting those flying sparks. His intervention ensured Jacob graduated with his classmates.

As the cab drew near Park Square, Galloway patted the side and disembarked. He preferred to walk the last mile home, no matter the weather. He approached his terrace home from the south, as was his custom. A soft, yellow glow shone through the parlour window. Lakshmi had the boys there with her, no doubt, amusing them until bedtime.

A cough drew Galloway's attention to the corner of the street. Four men stood together in a crude circle. One clenched a clay pipe between his teeth, an ugly flare of matchlight illuminated their faces for a moment. All four wore hats and two sported moustaches. He didn't recognise them, nor did they look like residents. He considered for a moment asking if they were lost, then thought better of it.

"I say, Jake! You're home a bit late this evening, aren't you?"

The hail came from the steps of the neighboring terrace house. Galloway set his jaw. He was a Scotsman and so 'Jake' was better than the alternative 'Jock' but he disliked both nicknames. He also disliked being watched with such interest. A clear sign it was time to change his routine and keep it varied.

"How are you, Charles?" Galloway asked, manufacturing a smile. As with most evenings, Grey smelt halfway into his cups already.

Grey lowered his voice and took a step closer to Galloway. "Those four have been there since half six, maybe longer." He gestured towards Galloway's house with his chin. "Shmi and the boys all right?"

Jacob's jaw set a little tighter, but he forced the smile to remain glued in place. The familiarity with which he'd been addressed grated on his nerves, and the addition of Lakshmi's diminutive served to annoy him and spread distance between them. Galloway supposed Grey's time in India lent an air of kindred spirits. Judging by gossip, Grey had several children by Indian women, none of whom he'd brought back with him.

"As far as I know, she and the boys are fine. Not that I've been in to see them yet." And the strange men might have their names now, thanks to Grey's loudmouth and penchant for not keeping it in check. Perhaps 'fine' was not the correct word.

Grey stepped in closer, appearing to shift his weight casually. At this distance, the man stank like a distillery, and Galloway held his breath again.

"They've been watching your house, I think. Looking to burgle it, I suppose," Grey said, voice too low to carry. "I've been standing lookout as best I could without arousing suspicion, but it's your place they keep glancing at, not mine." Grey shrugged. "Then again, with me on the doorstep, it's difficult to be certain."

Galloway looked at the parlour window again, then back at Grey. Uneasiness coiled tight in his midsection, like when he'd stepped into a nest of venomous snakes. Heavy leather boots and unseasonably cool weather had saved his skin that time, but what grace of God was there this time?

"And they've only been here since half-six, no earlier?"

"I don't know. It may have been longer, and I didn't see them until then."

A slow, tickling nag began in the back of Galloway's mind, like a half-remembered song. He was worried over nothing, surely. Four strangers on the corner were unusual, suspicious even, but no cause for panic.

"Did Lakshmi take the boys out for their walk this afternoon?"

Grey looked up, eyes glazed and rheumy from drink. There was an ugly, savage little glare beating out from behind the red-snapped blue. It was there for a moment, then gone. "I can't rightly say, old boy. I wasn't watching that closely. She does most days, doesn't she?"

"Most days," Galloway agreed. He looked at the group of strangers again, the fine hairs on his neck standing up. Just the wind, he told himself, the wind on the back of that infernal rain. Nothing more. "Go on in," Grey said, patting Jacob's arm. "I'll stand here a bit."

Despite his ever-growing disquiet, Galloway nodded and turned. Although his lifted chin and straight back suggested he was shut of the matter, he wasn't. The men haunted his thoughts; Grey haunted his thoughts. What was that fleeting fury?

He undid the latch and let himself inside the house, careful to lock the door behind him. Two small forms shot out from the parlour, one clutching each of his legs. Jacob grunted but weathered the assault and managed to stay upright. Rahul was six and Frederick was four. Still small enough not to knock him over, but big enough to upset his balance.

Lakshmi emerged, also smiling, and helped take Galloway's cloak. "They heard you talking outside. It pained them to wait," she said, brushing droplets of rain off the cloak before hanging it on the rack. "Was it Mister Grey who stopped you?"

He turned, pinwheeling his arms to avoid losing his balance altogether. Galloway watched his wife for a moment, feeling his smile fade like a sunset. In the right company, his composure was implacable, but not with her. With Shmi, composure fell away and left him.

"It was Grey, yes, but…" Galloway trailed off, weighing whether he wanted to proceed. "But why do you ask? No one else stops me in the evenings."

Lakshmi drew away Frederick so her husband could walk. Rahul took his father's forearm but remained silent, awaiting his turn to speak. It occurred to Jacob he had to be careful what he said and how he said it, lest he scare the children. His own mother was often fearful and her fear had sometimes infected him. He didn't want to do that to them.

"We kept dinner for you," Lakshmi said, motioning him to the dining room. "I suppose it is dried out now, but perhaps it will still taste nice."

Galloway's stomach rumbled audibly as the aroma of dinner grew the closer they grew to the table and both boys giggled at the noise. Jacob smiled at them and winked.

"Yes, I'm sorry I'm late. I don't know why Mister Robinson asks me for things on the way out every night, but what can I do?" The Company had sent Galloway back to London for the specific purpose of working on quinine treatments for at-risk Company workers, as such, they guarded his time like dragons over treasure. But as much as Galloway wanted to brush off Robinson, he was the boss's son and demanded attention.

He tucked into the samosa she'd prepared. They were not dry despite his delay to the table. Potatoes, peas, chutney, and garam marsala danced over his tongue. After several bites, he recalled what he'd been trying to ask her before dinner sidetracked him.

"Why did you ask if I was talking to Mister Grey?" he asked, setting down his food to meet her eyes.

Laki sat down in the seat beside him, an unorthodox and charming choice, offset by her hesitation. She looked from Frederick to Rahul, then back again to Jacob. He wondered if she had the same misgivings he did, about frightening the children.

"Your voice was nearby so I supposed you had to be talking to him," she said. The words came so slowly that Galloway considered asking her to try in Hindi. But her English was better than his Hindi, so it wasn't a language issue. More likely, she was holding back something for the sake of the boys, just as he was.

"Rahul, take Frederick to the parlour, please," Galloway told the older boy. "We'll join you shortly then put you to bed."

"But, Father, we—"

It was difficult to refuse the big, hazel eyes but Jacob shook his head 'no'. He knew they were tired, but this was not the time for acting out. Seeing their father's grave expression, the children didn't press and withdrew as instructed.

Once the parlour doors clicked closed, he pushed away his plate and took Lakshmi's hand. She clutched it back, squeezing his fingers so hard, the tips began to turn white.

"There are men in the neighbourhood," she said. "All this week, maybe before but I didn't notice them. Strangers. Whenever the boys and I go out to walk, they're here. On the street, on the corner." Lakshmi held her breath, then let it out slowly. "It may be nothing. English men on English streets are not so strange, but they stare so, and they look out of place. It made me wonder if they'd stopped you to talk."

He took up her other hand in his and leaned forward to kiss her fingers. The British Company paid its men to father children with as many Indian women as possible, then to leave them behind to 'improve' the population.

They were not encouraged to marry or bring them home but were semi-encouraged to send the boys back to England under assumed names for schooling.

This was not a philosophy that sat well with Galloway, so he'd done the opposite: he'd married the woman he loved and brought her back to England (temporarily, at least). Their first-born shared the name of Lakshmi's brother and Galloway did not regret it. However, their choices were not regarded well by everyone.

They were fortunate their neighbour, Mister Grey, was tolerant and even friendly. Another British Company man like Galloway, perhaps he'd left behind someone he didn't want to abandon, who knew? Many Company men shunned Galloway and his family, a fact which troubled him not at all. Good riddance to them. He'd faced expulsion from college for not subscribing to backwards thinking and superstition, damned if he was going to start now.

"I noticed a quartet of men as I walked up tonight," Galloway said. It was his turn to speak slowly and now he understood. Lakshmi had tried to choose her words with care, not wanting to alarm him any more than necessary. His mission was the same. "I understand what you mean, I didn't like the look of them either, they seem out of their element. Mister Grey seemed to think they were surveying houses to rob."

There was a long pause as Lakshmi looked at him, searching his face for falsehood. After several seconds, she seemed satisfied in his honesty and straightened.

"Is there anything we can do, Coby?" she asked, the death grip on his fingers relaxing slightly. "Should we tell the police?"

A noise came from his throat, some sort of contemplative but uncertain 'mmm' sound before he spoke. "We could tell the night watchman, then see the police on High Street in the morning."

The coil of uneasiness returned to his midsection, tightening with each word. Laki's downturned eyes expressed the same doubt as his tone. The night watchman was elderly, often drunk, and allegedly took a few shillings in exchange for a blind eye to unsavoury nighttime activities.

"We'll wait until morning," she said.

Galloway nodded in support of her decision. He trusted her judgement. Her experience as an Indian woman in England was difficult and unpleasant. Delhi had challenges for her and for their sons, but those challenges were understood and quantifiable. Lakshmi was not alien there and her family seemed to view their marriage as honourable. His acceptance and pride in the boys had won him their favour. Although they were uncertain about light-eyed, fair-haired Rahul, they did not mistreat him.

Acte Deux.

In England, the couple had no friends and she was regarded like a tiger: beautiful, exotic, and savage. So, if she wanted to avoid the night watchman, there was a reason that was likely due to her treatment, or the treatment of their sons. The watchman had been either lascivious or callous, no doubt, although Laki had not mentioned it.

While Lakshmi removed the dinnerware, Jacob retired to the parlour and visited with the boys. At last, the evening took on its usual tones and he relaxed. They played a few rounds of Crambo at the children's behest until the warmth of the fire did its work. Once Frederick's eyes began to slip closed, Galloway picked him up and ushered his brother upstairs for bed. When they were finally tucked away, he looked out the window one more time. The corner where the quartet of men had been was now vacant, and it looked like Grey's house was dark. Lakshmi stood beside him.

"It seems quiet now."

"It does. And I don't see anyone, do you?"

Rather than answer immediately, she took time to examine the outdoors carefully before replying. It was one of the things he loved about her, that thoughtful consideration she gave everything.

"No, there is nothing. Perhaps I misjudged. And I'm sorry, Coby, I should have told you sooner, but I thought I was imagining things. Overreacting."

"If you misjudged, then I did too," Galloway said. She was not a rash woman and her instincts were good. Add to that his own misgivings and he thought misjudging what they saw was the least likely explanation. What bothered him most was that these strange men had been sniffing about for days, which suggested they'd be back again. He sighed. "At any rate, they're gone for now. Let's retire and bring it to the police tomorrow. For peace of mind, if nothing else."

After a thin, restless sleep, morning light did not improve Galloway's uneasiness. He thought it might. Nighttime monsters had a way of looking less frightening by the light of day, but not this time. If anything, he felt more unsettled than before. He supposed it was because work would call him away for the day when he'd prefer to be home, keeping watch.

Once they'd eaten and the boys were dressed, Galloway sent a message to the office that he would be late due to a police matter. They took a cab to the police station on High Street. Frederick was fascinated by the police in their uniforms, especially enamoured with the tall hats and long coats. One of the officers smiled at the darker complexioned boy, but most did not.

Fortunately, Doctor Galloway the senior was somewhat Moorish in complexion himself, and an influential man in both Edinburgh and London. The Marylebone police had no choice but to be civil.

"And it's four men you say, Doctor Galloway?"

This was the third time they'd been asked that same question and he lost another sliver of patience. The constable wasn't stupid; he was either trying to trip them up or cause them grief.

"Yes, it was four men. They all had hats, three were brown hats, one was black. Two had moustaches, one had about three days' worth of beard growing in. I couldn't make out colours on their lower halves because it was nightfall."

"Their trousers were all soiled so it was difficult to discern colours," Lakshmi said. "I saw these men several times when the boys and I took our afternoon outings. One has a red kerchief around his neck and smokes a clay pipe. Another is flaxen haired and was in a fight." She held up a hand and covered her right eye. "This side was swollen earlier in the week, so it must still be bruised."

The constable made some notes, then nodded. "We'll have a constable come round on foot tonight, make sure everything is all right."

"Tonight? What about this afternoon? They've been on the street at all hours of the day and night."

"Won't your neighbour, Mister…Grey be on watch in the meantime?"

Jacob's patience slipped further, and his face began to warm. He did not anger easily or often, but he was well on his way there. "He may be available, but I daresay it's not Mister Grey's job to guard my home whilst I'm out for the day. What was the point of the police reform if this sort of laziness is the outcome? Because that wouldn't have happened a few years back, I can assure you."

Lakshmi put her hand on his forearm, resting the other on Frederick's back to quell his disquiet. Their father didn't raise his voice often.

It was the constable's turn for a red face, only he was red from embarrassment rather than temper. He mumbled something that Galloway couldn't hear and excused himself. Jacob grunted in disgust and stood. He was spoilt, he supposed, used to getting his way and more simply because he was a Galloway. Being singled out for the appearance and background of his family was a new and uncomfortable experience.

"Come along then," he said, finding a smile and some cheer for his tone. "We'll have Mister Grey check in on you this afternoon, how does that sound?"

"Could he play Charades with us, Papa?" Rahul asked, taking his brother's hand. "He's ever so good at it."

Jacob puffed air from his lips, a weak laugh, but a laugh just the same. They made it difficult to stay angry. "Mister Grey plays Charades with you? Really?" He shook his head. "The things that go on in our home that I don't know about, I swear."

"He stops in sometimes and he's always very kind," Lakshmi said, slipping on her gloves. "And he's patient with the boys—listens to them, likes to play with them. He said once he always wanted children of his own."

Galloway considered pointing out that he had plenty of them, they were just all left behind in India, then he thought better of it.

. Just because he was ill-tempered didn't mean he had to spread it about.

Jacob ushered his family outside and hailed a cab. One didn't stop even though it was empty, but the next did. Once they were headed back, he resumed the discussion.

"It's fine, I'll stop by Charles's house for a moment on my way to the office and ask him to look in on you all. It might be wise to stay inside today, as well, so there's no fixed routine for them to seize on."

With the family sorted, Galloway knocked on Grey's door. No answer. Odd but not entirely unexpected. He'd already reeked of gin by eight o'clock last night and might have continued drinking long after. But Galloway had no time to tarry and tucked a calling card in the door, folding the corner to request Grey's visit in person. He'd never done that before in the entirety of their acquaintance, so hopefully the urgency would be understood.

He arrived at work around midday and the earlier sun slipped behind cloud cover. Jacob took a moment to check in with Mister Robinson (senior, not junior), then headed down to the laboratories.

Robinson (junior, this time) also stopped by. Galloway wondered if something about him seemed off because after only a few minutes of chatting, Robinson Junior put a hand on his shoulder.

"Listen, Galloway, I've never seen you like this. Why don't you go home and spend time with your family. We'll see you back here on Monday morning."

"I'm fine."

"You're absent-minded and irritable and just came in from the police. You're not 'fine'," Robinson said. "I don't know what's happened, but I do know you're valuable to us. Take the afternoon, take the weekend, come back to us on Monday."

Jacob started to protest, his temper rearing its head again, then swallowed it all back. Mister Robinson was right. This wasn't like him. He didn't take excessive personal time and he was worried about his family. Probably without cause, but still worried.

He nodded and held out his hand to shake Robinson's. "Thank you. I'll be back first thing Monday."

Back outdoors, rain pattered onto the stones, releasing a sickly wet stink of the city–of mildew, aged dung, and the layers of filth generated by burgeoning industry. Galloway pulled up his collar and hailed the first cab he saw.

Since he travelled alone now, a good-looking blond fellow leaving a prestigious office, he had no trouble flagging down a driver.

The ride back seemed longer than usual, that ball of worry in his belly was spreading again, tightening like a fist. The strange men watching his home left him more uneasy than he'd realised. Every minute seemed drawn out into an hour. As anxious as he was to get home, he dreaded it too. There was some unspeakable fear of what he might find when he got there.

Acte Final.

As the cab rolled closer, the air changed its smell from a wet, mossy stink to something crisp. Probably the neighbourhood fireplaces working against the rainy chill. He looked out the door of the cab and saw nothing unusual, just the smell of wood smoke stronger than usual. But as the cab drew closer to the row of terrace houses, the smell grew heavier. His heartbeat faster in his chest, the sense of misgiving that was a tickle last night was a full-on roar now.

A column of smoke drifted up into the air, much too thick to be from chimneys, and Galloway lept from the cab, almost tripping on his way down. His house. It was his house on fire, he knew it.

And sure enough, when he rounded the corner, he saw a group of men with torches raised aloft shouting some incomprehensible crowd noises. He supposed there were words in the shouts but he couldn't make out any of them. At least four of the men were the strangers he'd seen the night before, the men Lakshmi described to the police.

Grey was there too, shouting, torch raised aloft with the others. Galloway grabbed his neighbour's shoulder and spun him round so they were face to face. He was red again, he could feel it, eyes stinging with tears from rage and smoke. Flames crawled and licked from the first and second floor windows of his home and he knew with a sinking nausea, that all hope was lost for his family. The fire raged so violently that there was no saving them now. None.

"What are you doing, you bloody fool? Your house will burn too!" Jacob's mouth worked, there were so many things he wanted to scream in the bastard's face before beating it into an unrecognisable pulp, but all words failed.

The tears ran freely down his face now and he lifted Grey up by the collar. "You were supposed to take care of them, damn it! What's wrong with you?"

Grey's face twisted and Galloway saw that ugly flare in his eyes again, although it didn't go away this time. He still stank of gin and sweat and he slapped Jacob's hands away from his collar as though the chemist were made of faeces.

"You're a disgusting pig, Galloway. You're all disgusting pigs. You don't deserve to live here with your coolie woman and chee-chee brats. This is an English neighbourhood, a *good* neighbourhood. You don't belong here, any of you, and you never did."

As the house continued to burn, more open-mouthed gapers came to watch the spectacle. Jacob's mouth moved again, open-closed, open-closed, like a fish dying in a new universe called 'land'. He'd never especially liked Grey, no, but he'd never suspected this. Never this.

Inside his burning home, he thought he heard a small cry, but with the smoke belching forth, it was probably just his mind playing tricks on him.

"They never did anything to you," he said, voice growing harsh as he drew in smoke. "They were just living."

Grey's lips drew back from his teeth. "You, you think you're better than everyone else with your company commission and your father always pulling you out of trouble. You think you can do whatever you want, say whatever you want. Well, I'll tell you something, Jacob Galloway, you're just a man like I am." Grey's voice was cracking too, tears squeezing out of his eyes now as well, presumably from the smoke, but with the insanity he was spewing, it might have been something else. Jacob didn't know anymore. "You're not special. Today and every day after, you'll remember that you're not special, that you don't deserve anything better than the rest of us. When your gut is rotting out with grief and drink, then you'll know what it's like."

"You're mad," Galloway said, but it sounded more like a dog's snarl than proper words. He seized Grey by the collar again and hit him this time, fist closed and moving so fast, it seemed to whistle. Grey's head snapped back as though his neck were a spring and Galloway felt a sick satisfaction spread through his gut. "You could've helped and you killed them instead."

"I did. I set fire to the curtains right in front of them. They cried and they begged and I locked them upstairs in the bedrooms so they couldn't get out. You should've heard them, Galloway. It sounded like pigs squealing in a slaughterhouse."

Jacob glanced up, unable to help himself. The windows were all broken, downstairs and up, whether from escape attempts or sheer heat, he couldn't tell. In the distance, he heard the engines finally approaching. They were coming from Baker Street way, he thought, but didn't know for sure and didn't care. It didn't matter now, all was lost.

He hit Grey again, and felt his knuckles make contact with teeth. The flesh split and then pain seemed to explode beneath that. The ache was immediate and tremendous, but almost welcome. It gave him something else to focus on. That and the satisfaction of seeing Grey's face swollen and bleeding. At that moment, Jacob didn't care if he went to gaol or even if he died. In fact, the latter seemed like a comforting idea. He'd rather die than live without his family.

Twelve years and four thousand miles away, Galloway gasped awake. A memory–a nightmare lived still in the wee hours of the night–he gulped in the thick perfumed air as he oriented. His neck and hips groaned like rusted metal and tears burnt behind his eyelids, pain equal partners with grief. Time had drifted by in a haze of smoke and regret but the restless ghosts of his family lingered.

He fumbled for his journal, determined to write no matter how his throat quivered or how his hands shook. Crumpled inside the dirty leather satchel was an unopened envelope. He'd intended to read the message earlier, but nodding off had a way of affecting one's plans and never for the better.

In the pale glow of the opium den, he examined it again, noting The British Company's seal and the sender's name, Colonel R.C. Stevens. What could The Company want with him after all this time? It was a mystery just interesting enough to pique his curiosity.

Doctor Galloway,

King, Country, and Company command your service.

Plan to arrive two days hence. Require your aid investigating strange black mass.

More details to be provided upon your arrival at interior camp Imbokko.

-Col. R.C. Stevens

One of Jacob's fellow smokers stirred (no small feat whilst in a haze) and he realised he'd growled. The note sat in his first, crumpled intentionally this time. He started to toss it into the dying fire, then palmed it back into the satchel.

Maybe this was the opportunity he'd been awaiting. Maybe this time, things would work out in his favour. The Company had newer scientists, younger scientists, but was calling upon him. Either they were desperate and wouldn't say so, or had need of a more experienced hand.

Perhaps this was his chance to shine one last time.

GRAND GUIGNOL

MIMES

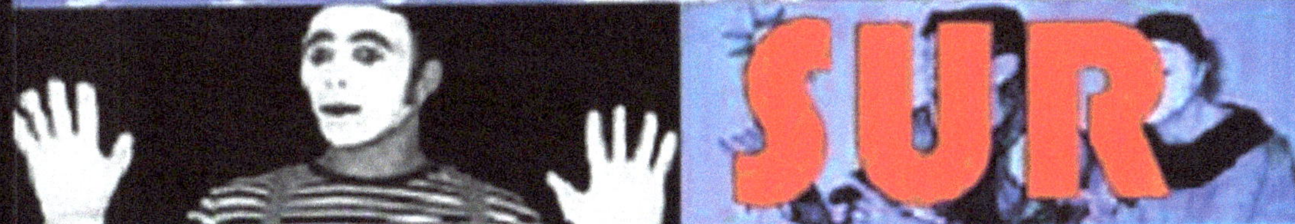

le EXPLOSIF finale!!! violence! CARNAGE! mimes?

LE GRAND EXPLOSIF!

Une Nuit au Theatre du Grand Guignol

Piece en un acte.

Paris, March 6, 1921.

A mild end to winter, before spring brings its splendor, L'Artiste rises from his bed on the ground. The shanty surrounding him is adequate. He gathers his makeup and begins his early morning routine. The spread of the grease paint, the single black tear against the bone white smear of makeup. He does not speak. Cannot speak. The day he cut his tongue and severed his vocal cords with that invisible sword was the day he became the Truest Mime. L'Artiste.

He doesn't recall his name before that day. Nor does he wish to recall.

L'Artiste takes care to present his cleanest self, washing his clothes by nightfall in the Seine but the winters were harsh–it shows on his threadbare trousers. But still, he walks, head held high, to the park. A show goes on. It must go on. With every deliberate step, he bears down on the park. They will laugh, and clap, and throw him their spare change. A lad who wants to impress his lady will give whole notes to him, and he will eat tonight.

He ignores the growling in his gut, though he can hear it (and surely others could too). That would ruin his act! L'Artiste passes a café and with a single deft move, removes a bag of pain au chocolat off a distracted businessman and makes his exit. The pastry is devoured and the bag discarded before anyone even notices

L'Artiste, content with his morning cadge, smiles as he enters the park. His smile falters, however, to see that someone has taken his spot. His act. His bread and butter.

That BOUFFON.

A fellow mime, one would say. If L'Artiste could say anything, he would say Le Bouffon is the slime that runs out of the shantytown each morning. A river of shit, snot, and piss as les miserables turn out each morning to beg, steal and borrow their ways through the days.

Fellow mime. Wretch. Too colorful, this one, too magenta and pink with his polka-dot suit and his papier-mache banana in place of a flower on his lapel. Disgusting. A mere clown with a mime act!

There was hardly a crowd gathered around Le Bouffon but it was not his rightful crowd. No, that crowd belonged to him, L'Artiste! How dare–how very dare he.

With a smug side-eye, Le Bouffon gave a grin to L'Artiste. This was certainly the best way to antagonize his truest enemy, the mime. This mime–the one people called L'Artiste.

Le Bouffon, a silent clown who could not speak after drinking an invisible gallon of what he thought was water, only later to find out it was hydrofluoric acid, took L'Artiste's spot once he found that this was the prime spot for passers-by.

How he did not die from his invisible poison was a mystery for the ages. The only thing Le Bouffon could imagine was that he had eaten some invisible, mystical antidote beforehand and survived the necrosis of his vocal cords. All this only served to ensure him that his remaining on this plane of existence was to serve as his foil to this perverted mime.

Mimes, the perversion of clowns. Vile, base creatures, the lot.

And L'Artiste was the last mime in existence. The final target.

Le Bouffon continued his rope climb of the invisible mountain, sometimes appearing to lift off the ground with both feet, delighting the children who clapped their hands and the parents donating what little spare change they had.

Suce ma bite, L'Artiste. Oh if only!

He could not risk an accidental show in his polka-dot pants with that thought, and concentrated on the apex of the mountain. Almost there, a little slip here, a little trip there. Up and up, the crowd amassed to see the terrible trial of dominating the tallest mountain on the planet.

WHOMP.

A blur of a black and white striped shirt and black pants, L'Artiste tackled Le Bouffon, and down the invisible mountain they went. Le Bouffon rolled on top of L'Artiste as they tumbled to the ground. The children laughed at the sight of the beret, glued to L'Artiste's head, flapping and flopping around, but not coming off. Le Bouffon's hair, thick and lustrous black, betraying his Mediterranean or possibly Iberian heritage, stood in stark opposition to the bald and smooth white skull of L'Artiste. It coalesced into a bizarre Yin-Yang as they rolled around in what was fast becoming the muddy ground.

Punches thrown, a river of red ran down Le Bouffon's split lip. What? Impossible! A mime throwing and landing a solid hit to his finely chiseled clown face? Rude.

The split lip did not slow Le Bouffon as he attempted to rip the beret off L'Artiste's head and beat him with it. However, L'Artiste, spry and long-limbed, disentangled himself, moving well out of Le Bouffon's grasp.

A man known only as The Founder, led his group through the park. On their way to Le Théâtre du Grand-Guignol, a stop in the Park seemed like a lovely idea. He turned to his friend and smiled. "Here–this is the real show. Let's stay a while."

The Viscountess of the Quill nodded. After all, they'd unlocked the secret of Time Travel with his nanoscopic bots and her experiments with psychotropics. Why not stay a bit? They turned to their troupe of talent, Viscountess reaching out for the hand of the Viscount of the Real. "Let's look at what's drawing them all in."

Eldritch Deity not far behind, they came back to the troupe and pointed toward the roving Yin-Yang of struggle.

"Oh, a fight," The Slinger of Inks said. The troupe moved in closer, joined by the others–The Whispered Storm (La Musietta), The Speaker to Mistrals, Purveyor of Change, The Lyricist, and the Magician (also known to some as the Silent Partner).

As they gathered, pushing past the crowd, they bore witness to the possible extinction of the mime. The last of his kind.

Fists of rage, Le Bouffon cracked the jaw of L'Artiste, but the mime stayed strong, gnashing his teeth and clamping down on Le Bouffon's hand. A crunch sound came from the knuckles, but no sound came from either L'Artiste nor Le Bouffon. Tears streamed down their faces, but the grease paint didn't fade.

The crowd, led by the time traveling troupe, followed the fight across the park to the Eiffel Tower as the two rolled and attempted to slay one another.

Le Bouffon and L'Artiste kicked and punched their way to the elevator of the Eiffel Tower, clearing a path as people jumped out of their way. Either slay or be slain, the two embroiled in the pugilistic contest for survival didn't care if anyone else was pulled into the entanglement.

"Oh look, an organ grinder and his little monkey," The Lyricist said, gesturing to the two. Her eyes went wide as she saw the clowns tumbling towards them. "Watch out!"

The organ grinder stopped playing his tune and the monkey, looking to collect the money, saw the tussle and panicked, jumping into the elevator just as the two tumbled in. A flip of the switch, and the three were gone, carrying the organ grinder up and up until the tension of the leash became too great. SNAP.

The organ grinder fell to the ground, but rolled away with grace, as the Magician saw to it to provide a mattress from what seemed like thin air. It was a thin air mattress, and enough to break his fall.

Even though the fight was no longer visible as the monkey, the mime, and the clown rose to the top, a chihuahua, known by the name of Fifi Superb, scrambled up to see if anyone had scraps for her.

That's when she barked–a sharp yet lower-pitched bark that alerted people to the incoming danger. The incoming danger from high above.

Le Lamantin Dirigeable, known to Anglophones as The Airship Manatee, floated with enormous grace through the bright blue March sky. The pilot, a gaunt and grave looking man named Emilien Dubois, flew the enormous skyship over beautiful Paris.

"She handles like a pregnant whale," Emilien said, complaining to anyone within earshot. He grumbled as he steered through the sky. He should have been a scientist, said his mother. No, he wanted to scrape the sky with the future of travel. The Airship.

What a dirge this career had become. Instead of flying a majestic airbus, he was flying a tribute to the cow of the sea.

Emilien despised cows.

The hatred of Le Lamantin Dirigeable grew inside him over the months he'd been piloting this hideous blob, and the only coping skill that Emilien knew lay at the bottom of his wine bottle. Night after night, he would crawl into the bouteille and dream of gamma rays and their effect on water lilies.

After many nights of these journeys to the bottom of the wine glass, Dubois discovered he was better off bypassing the hangover by taking a nip or two to work with him. Two became three, and so on until the stench of the fermented grape permeated his skin. "Clean yourself up," they told him in threatening tones.

So he did, and kept his job piloting the bloated beast. It would only last a week.

It was this day that Emilien woke up and found himself alone in the dark, his assignment to fly Le Lamantin Dirigeable over Paris to London, and back again. And back again. And again. And again.

A bottle on the table, slipped into his carryall, and missing by the time he boarded the airship. He took flight, weaving upward, skyward. The baguette sloshed around in his stomach, a meager breakfast swimming in the deep red sea.

"This is what hate is," Dubois said. L'hôtesse de l'air came by with drinks, and he imbibed. What would one more matter?

He adjusted for the shift in the wind, moving in closer to the Tower. The flight plan was to come in close and land nearby for unloading the passengers, picking up more for a journey to the City of Fog.

"This is the City of Frog, and I am a citizen," he said, then laughed. When the hostess came by again, he quieted. He couldn't let her know that he'd had more than just one drink.

Balls.

There were balls–literal bright red balls–flying by the window of the airship. Dubois startled and jostled the controls, regaining control faster than his reflexes should have allowed him in his state.

But where were the balls coming from? He peered out the window, down to the tower, to see they were not balls, but balloons.

A tiny mime and a tiny clown were attempting to strangle each other with the balloon strings, from what he could tell high up on his manatee perch. Of keen eyesight, Dubois could even make out the pink and white polka dot jacket of the clown as he wrestled with the mime.

"We need a better view of this," Dubois said. This was irregular, yet he was compelled to give his passengers the thrill of their lives.

"Mesdames et Messieurs, if you direct your attention to the port side of our magnificent airship, you will see the most entertaining comedy. A pugilistic display of Le Bouffon et Le Mime."

The rest of the balloons scattered as both mime and clown tumbled, and the crowd inside the airship oohed and ahhed, clapping their hands and laughing at the spectacle.

As the airship overhead drew closer, L'Artiste let go of the rest of the balloons, realizing that Le Bouffon's strength was equal to his own.

. At the top of the tower, they were now in the precarious position of rolling off the edge whilst caught in their final entanglement.

Poison glares for one another as they continued to land blows on face, chest, and stomach, Le Bouffon brought his leg up, slamming into L'Artiste's divide. AGAIN.

L'Artiste's eyes filled with tears as he made the crying gesture, then gathered his strength to leg sweep the clown. The organ grinder's monkey screamed at them, possibly to stop, but more likely to keep the excitement going.

The crowd above and below remained, some with binoculars and others with opera glasses, catching the thrill of the tussle.

The Founder was sure to keep everyone around him safe, lest the mime and clown take their violence back to the crowd. The elevator was still at the top, but it was the keen eye of La Musietta that caught what was happening even higher than the tower.

Luck was on their side, because the Viscountess spotted it as well. "That Airship–it's getting too close to the Tower," she said. Her maternal instincts kicked in and she held out one arm as if to ward them away from the potential danger.

The Founder could sense it, too. Danger was coming, though he couldn't see the specifics. Troupe of Talent combined, the group moved away to a safer vantage point where they could enjoy the spectacle without putting themselves in the middle of the action.

High above, L'Artiste et Le Bouffon rolled back onto the elevator, and the obedient monkey pulled at the lever, bringing them back down.

So amused by the spectacle below them, the sloshed pilot helped himself to another drink from the hostess. He leaned down to get a better look below, laughing aloud at the silly monkey that was dancing around on top of the back of L'Artiste, who was now cramming an invisible flower into the mouth of Le Bouffon.ajestic metal so casually, and she defended

Another gust of wind blew overhead, pushing the Airship farther and faster than it had any right to go. Flames fell in long tendrils as the huge manatee, as if propelled now by sheer will alone, made its way towards the Seine.

L'Artiste, dodging what looked like a flaming wine glass with a hand still around it, picked up a non-flaming severed head (singed) and proceeded to beat Le Bouffon with it.

As they rolled across towards the Seine, with the blimp floating high above them (lowering by the second), Le Bouffon took his advantage.

He pulled an invisible pistol from his inner coat pocket, and pressed it against the heart of L'Artiste.

Bang! The pistol went off and the crowd dispersed, some running to the bridge as if to visit the Louvre, some closer to L'Hotel des Invalides to worship and beg their god to show them mercy.

L'Artiste's eyes widened as the pain and heat of the slug penetrated his chest. He could not cry out, but the last of the mimes did mimic an agonized scream. Arms and legs flailing, he hit the water behind him with a great splash. Le Bouffon took a bow, dodging another ball of flame, and smiled.

A wide grin with tears in his eyes as he bid adieu to the last mime. A clown's victory that he would savor for years to come.

Sinking.

Not just the sensation of sinking, but literal sinking. L'Artiste's splash into the water pulled him inward into his own body. A lifetime of using his entire corporeal form to entertain and delight gave him insight into what he thought were his final moments.

The embrace of oblivion would come soon. He could feel it. His heart, penetrated by the slug, let out wispy tendrils of blood into the dirty Seine. Eyes open, mouth still an O of shock, L'Artiste sank. The weight of the slug felt too heavy, impossibly so, and the air left his lungs.

Yet it was not the slug or lack of air weighing him down. It was hands. Hands pulling him down.

Though no breath remained in his body, he was still breathing. Still conscious. It was to be so. He was no scientist and had no explanation for any of it. *Ce qui sera sera.*

A cheerful noise from the bottom of the Seine called to his muffled ears. A song, perhaps. One not yet written, not yet played. He knew the tune, and sang along in French. *L'avenir n'est pas à nous de voir! Ce qui sera sera! Ce qui sera sera!* Violins played in his mind and the cupid's bow mouth formed a smile.

What a lovely way to end it–what a beautiful tribute to the last of the mimes.

The darkness came over L'Artiste in an ever-narrowing tunnel. It was time to sleep at the bottom of the river. He would take his final rest there, and thought that perhaps he would wake soon, and exact his revenge on Le Bouffon.

He could still feel the hands on him, dragging him into the eternal *berceuse de l'univers*, the lullaby of the universe. The fire inside him did not dwindle but smoldered. The hands wrapped around his limbs, his waist, his neck, and pulled him to the bottom.

Ce qui sera.

Overhead, the Airship Manatee made its final descent, carrying the burnt remains of screaming, suffering passengers, who had begged their psychopathic god for mercy only to find no answers, or rather an answer of the inferno. It was as if their god had given them a mocking laugh in reply.

The tunnel came down to surround L'Artiste's vision and turned to a bright orange glow. It engulfed the waters overhead as he sank further into the river. His back grazed the surface of the riverbed, and the hands caressed him into a sweet slumber.

The slumber was not eternal, not even to last as long as the first two sections of Langgaard's *Music of the Spheres.*

"Terrible," The Founder said. "Should I say the thing I'm thinking?" He was eating popcorn as the troupe took in the show all around them.

"Mais oui," The Viscountess said with a lopsided smile. "Do it."

"You could say it's all up in flames," he said. "Hiyooooooo!"

The troupe tittered and a couple of them groaned at the pun, meandering away from the central danger. Their job was to observe, after all, not disturb what went on around them. Plus–to be injured or leave any sort of permanent mark would be unacceptable.

They set up a lovely picnic in their bubble, making a small mound upon which they could perch, drinking their favored beverages and foods as they recorded their observations. Chaos surrounded but did not penetrate their sphere of protection.

Giving a vantage point of the late afternoon sky, the troupe watched the fight as the crowd surged and the flaming Airship Manatee began its final descent. The sun began its own descent in concert. Time spent observing the fight meant that time did not stand still–it sped its way through the sky as the fight came to its end and L'Artiste appeared to breathe his last under the languid crawl of the Seine. A fast-paced, slow motion fall to the horizon, and to the depths of the riverbed.

Then, tranquil.

The crowd heaved collective sighs as Le Bouffon stood at the edge of the river, chest puffed, triumphant and sure of his victory. A rivulet of blood trickled down the right side of his philtrum and covered his upper lip in a claret line. He licked the blood and grinned. A salty victory.

Le Bouffon looked down at the scene as les policiers approached to make sense of what they'd witnessed. The crowd around him, so thick and deep, the police could not push their way through them with their usual speed.

Though unable to blend in with the crowd, Le Bouffon could act shocked and dismayed with the best actors ever to have lived. He put his hands up to his face, and the smile metamorphosed to an oval of shock with eyes widened to enhance the surprise. *Well, quelle surprise!* The mime is dead!

A wave of sound–cries and screams–fell in a decrescendo throughout the crowd, until the wave passed the multitudes and silence enshrouded them. The police, two officers, bellowed for people to clear a path. They obeyed, ever silent.

"What is the meaning of this?" One policeman asked. "We must clear the crowd. The Airship Manatee, she is still falling!"

As if united by some universal synchronization, the crowd looked up, turning their heads to see the remains of the burning sea cow crash into the river. Its embers ignited over the waters, mixing with what CH4 and other flammable gasses emitted from the waste waters.

The Seine, as if crying out, began to boil.

Rolling and churning, the policemen, Le Bouffon, the observers, and the throngs watched in awe as the waters gave off a foul smelling steam. The sun dipped below the horizon, and night displayed the river in a red-orange glow.

One astute little child pointed to the river. "It's boiling and pushing out bodies!"

A few in the crowd laughed, either from nerves or amusement, the sound indistinguishable–but others screamed in terror. It wasn't the dead bodies that were scaring them, no, for many by then were hardened from The Great War and the broken bodies piled two to three meters high.

The terror came from what was emerging–not dead–animated.

Animated mimes, with their garish, waterlogged faces and bloated sausage fingers grabbing their way to the riverbank.

The silence broken, the crowd began to scream and flow away from the bank. The troupe, safe in their bubble of scientific witchcraft, watched them all surging, climbing over each other as the mimes poured onto the land.

Le Bouffon's eyes that had so perfectly mimicked surprise now expressed genuine horror and confusion for that which was rising. Hundreds, no, thousands of mimes emerging from a boiling river was not–could not be–possible.

Yet, there it was, through some sort of scientific collaboration of circumstance, the strangest effect. These mimes were not dead. They were directed. Purposeful. Vengeful.

The clown froze only for a moment as several of the mimes set their gazes upon him. This kicked him into movement, and Le Bouffon sprinted across the park, moving as quickly as he could. Perhaps he could fool them into thinking he'd popped into the Louvre. Oh yes, as if he would go in there to lose them–perhaps stop at the gift shop for a trinket or two. A souvenir to remember this night of a glowing orange sky, a flaming airship, and a thousand mimes set to their revenge.

The ones that were not settling to their chase of Le Bouffon were tearing through the crowd. Mimes were not stupid people, and these mimes knew to go through the police, first. A large mime rammed the panic whistle through the teeth of one officer while a gang of six mimes tore the other copper apart, starting with his throat.

Mimes were never known to discriminate, so no one in the crowd was safe. The mimes tossed the little child aside, however, so that they would not get trampled. They had no interest in the small ones–they would be the ones left to bear witness to this fateful day.

Members of the crowd ran in different directions to dodge the mimes, but these attempts were futile–the clever group of pantomimes had thought well ahead, surrounding the area with invisible walls that would deliver electric shocks to those who brushed up against it.

L'Artiste emerged from the Seine at last, taking in huge gasps of air, his eyes fresh and clear. They trained on Le Bouffon in an instant, seeing the clown duck through the hordes, angling for the Louvre.

The mime, the cleverest of them all, L'Artiste gave chase. Cherche Le Bouffon off to the side of the museum, past the unguarded gate (the guard left to give aid to the wounded, only to be fried by the electrified barrier). The chase ensued.

Le Bouffon hid in the shadows, but the bright colored suit served as a target, a beacon for L'Artiste to narrow his focus. He tunneled down on the clown, picking up speed as he ran, almost a blur. He ducked through the invisible crack in the pantomime barrier and tumbled into the shadows. He ran farther than he needed to, well past the clown and out of sight.

He waited, encasing the clown in his vision and holding him in the center, tunneling down until the blood of a thousand mimes boiled inside of him, calling for revenge.

Looking around, it seemed L'Artiste ran by him and around the corner. Then, nothing.

Le Bouffon sighed. He would remain in the dark, staying in shadow until the worst was over, then slip away.

A sharp pain interrupted his plans as he felt a giant knife slice him from his bottom to his collarbone, and he heard, inside his mind, the sound of a rotor saw. The pain burned, but did not last. His final impressions were of L'Artiste miming a buzz saw, and seeing the world in two halves.

L'Artiste mimicked silent laughter throughout the silent slaughter as he pulled the invisible saw through flesh and bone. With a diamond blade, it could cut through anything–because anything was possible in one's imagination. He managed to mangle the collar bone and keep moving, through the throat and up through the skull, until Le Bouffon was divided amongst himself.

Victorious, L'Artiste tossed the invisible saw to the ground (where it made a clattering sound somewhere in the aether), and ran back through the park. The troupe of observers had vacated the premises in the interim, and what was left of the scene was near silent.

Hushed. To L'Artiste the only sounds were the winds from the river, which now ran red, and faint cries of children. The mimes, satisfied in their slaughter for all those who mocked them in the streets, refusing to pay for performances, and who'd ever berated them, returned to the Seine, entering in silence en masse.

L'Artiste knew that this was where he would go, and soon, to meet his end. Yet he was not to be the last.

The child–the astute and clever child, who screamed one last scream that the Seine was boiling–stood silent. Watching the mimes descend.

No words would ever escape the child's mouth again. L'Artiste approached.

He handed the child a bright red carnation, and took out his last tin of pancake makeup from one deep pocket. With quick and knowing hands, he painted the child's face to create the perfect miniature mime.

Wordless, L'Artiste descended to the Seine.

APRES Le SPECTACLE:

Le Foundateur et La Vicomtesse

The theatre has emptied, "*A Night at the Grand Guignol"* Having concluded hours ago. It is dark, except for two or three stage lamps that have been left on. They cast angular shadows among the orchestra, balcony, and boxes that hint at the madness and the macabre that occupied the venue while the show went on.

A lone figure sits in the middle of the third row, doing nothing else but listening to a soft, yet somehow epic song. It is a familiar tune, one everyone knows, one everyone can at least sing the chorus. A door opens at the back of theatre, light pours in as if from the dimension where it is born before it enters the universe.

La Vicomtesse enters through the door and sees her friend still sitting in the theatre. The door closes behind her, and once again the space is blanketed in darkness. The chorus of the song begins as she approaches.

Just call me angel…

La VICOMTESSE: This seat taken?

Le FOUNDATEUR: It's a free theatre.

La VICOMTESSE: Mmmm, pretty sure we charged them twenty bucks or something, Wally.

La FOUNDATEUR: Was that all? Should have charged them more. You see that one guy start crying and run out the back door when that girl threw the plastic bag with the shrimp cocktail over the other ones' head? Couldn't tell if he was crying because of the strangling or

La VICOMTESSE: If it was from the smell of that rotten seafood!

They laugh together for a few moments, and then there is silence. *La Vicomtesse* pokes *Le Foundateur* in the cheek.

La FOUNDATEUR: OW! The fuck was that for?

Le VICOMTESSE: Just doing what the song said to do.

La FOUNDATEUR: **Pretty sure she said "touch", not "jab" or "poke", Lucienne.**

La VICOMTESSE: **This is Grand Guignol, sir. Hey.**

Le FOUNDATEUR: **What?**

La VICOMTESSE: **You gonna be okay?**

Le FOUNDATEUR: **Hunh? Yeah. Of course. I'm always okay.**

La VICOMTESSE: **In all the time I've known you, you're almost never okay. I meant…**

Le FOUNDATEUR: **Lucienne? I'll be fine. My Absolution approaches, closer and closer, even as we speak.**

La VICOMTESSE: **Will you tell me when it –**

Le Foundateur holds his arms straight in the air, and with imperceptible speed performs the dispelling gestures. The theatre vanishes, and the two of them are standing outside, in an alleyway, under a single streetlamp. The Heretics await at the entrance to the street, several yards away.

La VICOMTESSE: **arrives? You know I hate it when you do that.**
Le FOUNDATEUR: **Yep. And yes, I will.** ***Bon chance, ma soeur.***

La VICOMTESSE: **Kid, your French really sucks.** ***Toi aussi, petit frere.***

The two embrace for a moment. Le Foundateur turns to look down the alleyway to the group that awaits him, that await the next part of their journey.

Le FOUNDATEUR: **Besides, I got all these cats to look after so –**

Le Foundateur turns back to where La Vicomtesse had been standing, but she has vanished. He shakes his head and smiles.

Le FOUNDATEUR: **I hate it when she does that.**

Le Foundateur turns back down the alleyway, and walks into the darkness to meet his friends.

And slowly turn away…

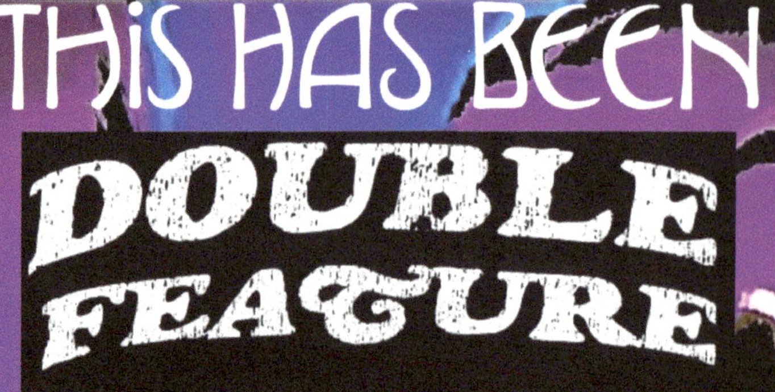

ANNUAL ISSUE #1:

"A Night at the Grand Guignol"

w p QUIGLEY
s n HUMPHREYS
Lucienne LEBEAU
d s VERNON
Melody ALICE
john a. McCOLLEY
Madi QUINN
Michael STRONG
with Nix BLACK
and maggie MOREAU